IN THE ARMS OF LOVE

Barbara Cartland

Barbara Cartland Ebooks Ltd

This edition © 2018

ISBNs

9781788670876   EPUB

9781788670883   PAPERBACK

Book design by M-Y Books

m-ybooks.co.uk

THE BARBARA CARTLAND ETERNAL COLLECTION

The Barbara Cartland Eternal Collection is the unique opportunity to collect all five hundred of the timeless beautiful romantic novels written by the world's most celebrated and enduring romantic author.

Named the Eternal Collection because Barbara's inspiring stories of pure love, just the same as love itself, the books will be published on the internet at the rate of four titles per month until all five hundred are available.

The Eternal Collection, classic pure romance available worldwide for all time .

THE LATE DAME BARBARA CARTLAND

Barbara Cartland, who sadly died in May 2000 at the grand age of ninety eight, remains one of the world's most famous romantic novelists. With worldwide sales of over one billion, her outstanding 723 books have been translated into thirty six different languages, to be enjoyed by readers of romance globally.

Writing her first book 'Jigsaw' at the age of 21, Barbara became an immediate bestseller. Building upon this initial success, she wrote continuously throughout her life, producing bestsellers for an astonishing 76 years. In addition to Barbara Cartland's legion of fans in the UK and across Europe, her books have always been immensely popular in the USA. In 1976 she achieved the unprecedented feat of having books at numbers 1 & 2 in the prestigious B. Dalton Bookseller bestsellers list.

Although she is often referred to as the 'Queen of Romance', Barbara Cartland also wrote several historical biographies, six autobiographies and numerous theatrical plays as well as books on life, love, health and cookery. Becoming one of Britain's most popular media personalities and dressed in her trademark pink, Barbara spoke on radio and television about social and political issues, as well as making many public appearances.

In 1991 she became a Dame of the Order of the British Empire for her contribution to literature and her work for humanitarian and charitable causes.

Known for her glamour, style, and vitality Barbara Cartland became a legend in her own lifetime. Best remembered for her wonderful romantic novels and loved by millions of readers worldwide, her books remain treasured for their heroic heroes, plucky heroines and traditional values. But above all, it was Barbara Cartland's overriding belief in the positive power of love to help, heal and improve the quality of life for everyone that made her truly unique.

AUTHOR'S NOTE

Although in England, unlike Scotland, succession to a title goes only in the male line, but there have, however, been exceptions.

The first and famous Duke of Marlborough under a special Act of Parliament was succeeded by his daughter, Henrietta, who became the second Duchess of Marlborough.

The Earl Mountbatten of Burma, who was assassinated in 1979 was under the same Act of Parliament succeeded by his daughter, Baroness Brabourne, who has become the Countess Mountbatten of Burma and her son will assume the title on her death.

CHAPTER ONE
1819

The Marquis of Thame watched his horses gallop past and turned with a smile of satisfaction to his friend Charlie Caversham.

"Two minutes, twenty seconds!" he exclaimed. "That is the fastest any horse I have ever owned has managed on this gallop."

"I told you that Red Duster was a winner when I first saw him," Charlie answered.

"I know you did," the Marquis replied, "but it never pays to be over-optimistic where horses or women are concerned."

They both laughed.

The Marquis put his watch into his pocket and walked away to find his trainer and congratulate him.

The Marquis had been exceedingly successful on the turf during the last year and he knew it was because he had sacked his old trainer and taken on a new man whose enthusiasm and ideas were proving almost sensational where his stable was concerned.

They had a long discussion on the various merits of all the horses that they had just watched on the gallop.

Then the Marquis and the Honourable Charles Caversham swung themselves onto the saddles of the two horses that they had ridden to the Newmarket

Downs on and began to ride back towards the Marquis's house.

It was on the outskirts of the small town, which was concerned entirely with the racing fraternity.

It was the Prince Regent who had originally made it clear that he greatly enjoyed coming to Newmarket and his lead had been followed, as it had been centuries before when King Charles II had said the same thing, by all the other owners so that Newmarket had grown from a small village into a thriving community.

The Marquis's house, which had been built by his father, was a long low building of mellow red bricks, which was not only admired by those who saw it but his guests found it one of the most comfortable of his many houses.

Exceedingly wealthy, besides bearing a distinguished name, the Marquis owned houses in many parts of England.

There was Thame, the main family seat, which was spoken of as being one of the finest and most outstanding country mansions built by Robert Adam.

It was impossible not to admire his Hunting Lodge in Leicestershire which was large enough to hold a party of fifty guests without overcrowding, his house at Ascot, which he occupied only during Race Week and, of course, his house in London situated in fashionable Berkeley Square.

His closest friend, Charles Caversham, reflected that perhaps the Marquis was most at home in

Newmarket simply because it was redolent of the sport he most enjoyed.

The room the two friends walked into when they entered the house was hung with pictures of racehorses by great artists and the leather chairs were in the dark green that was predominant in the Marquis's racing colours.

"Put your money on Red Duster, Charlie," the Marquis suggested, as he moved towards the drinks on the grog table.

"I have every intention of doing so," Charlie answered. "At the same time I think we ought to do it cleverly otherwise as usual your horse will become favourite and we shall be offered very short odds."

"I agree with you," the Marquis replied. "So the less we say about the results we saw this morning the better!"

He poured his friend out a glass of champagne and, as he took it, Charlie raised it to toast,

"To Red Duster. And may your proverbial good luck never grow less!"

"Thank you, Charlie," the Marquis smiled.

He refilled his friend's glass, but he poured very little into his own and, although Charlie noticed it, he said nothing, knowing how abstemious the Marquis was.

Extremely athletic the Marquis was proud of the fact that he could outride, out-box, out-shoot and out-fence all his friends, while a long day's hunting, which would often leave them exhausted, merely seemed to give him a new zest that it was impossible not to envy.

"Are we driving back to London this afternoon?" Charlie asked him.

"I don't know," the Marquis replied. "I have not yet made up my mind."

"About what?"

"Whether I should accept a very strange invitation."

"From whom?"

"I wanted to tell you about it last night," he answered, "but with all those people to dinner it was impossible. You may be able to enlighten me now on something that has been puzzling me for some time."

"It sounds mysterious."

Charlie grinned as he spoke, because he knew there was nothing the Marquis enjoyed more than something that was puzzling, difficult to understand or could not immediately be put into its proper category.

The two friends had fought at the Battle of Waterloo together and Charlie knew that, despite his wealth and being lionised by the raffish Society that circled around the Prince Regent, the Marquis was often bored.

He was too energetic and too vivid a personality to be content with Royal dinner parties or the innumerable beautiful women who pursued him relentlessly.

After the long War against Napoleon, despite the fact that prices were high and many people in the country were suffering from poverty and privation, the Social world celebrated peace with an outburst of balls, parties, *soirées*, Receptions, Assemblies and fireworks that succeeded each other night after night and inevitably after four years had become somewhat monotonous and repetitive.

The Marquis certainly diversified his interests between his addiction to sport and his lavish entertaining in his houses both in London and the country.

Equally Charlie often thought that there was something missing and he decided somewhat wryly that it was in fact the dangers of war that had given his friend an interest more exciting than anything that he found now that there was peace.

The Marquis walked to his desk and, putting down his glass of champagne almost untouched, picked up a letter that was heavily embossed with a Ducal crest.

He looked at it for a moment and then he asked,

"What do you know, Charlie, about the Duchess of Grimstone?"

"Quite a lot, as it happens," Charlie replied. "But I am surprised that you should have heard from her, if that is who your letter is from."

Holding the letter in his hand the Marquis sat down in a comfortable armchair opposite his friend as he went on,

"I will tell you what has happened and then I will be eager to hear anything you may be able to tell me."

"I am listening."

"The last time I was down here, about two months ago," the Marquis began, "my Agent, a stolid, rather uncommunicative man, surprised me by complaining volubly about things that were taking place on our boundary with the land belonging to the Duchess."

"Good Heavens! I had no idea of that," Charlie exclaimed.

"Apparently she owns a great deal of land, twenty thousand acres or more, North of Newmarket," the Marquis said, "much of it, I believe, wild and uncultivated with a few scattered villages."

Charlie nodded as if he was already aware of this, but he did not speak and the Marquis continued,

"According to Jackson, the Duchess's keepers and woodmen were behaving in an aggressive and quite unnecessarily harsh manner to my tenants and farmers."

"Why should they do so?"

"I did not think at the time that what Jackson told me was very important," the Marquis replied. "Farmers complained that if their cattle or sheep strayed they were never seen again. Dogs were shot if they ventured into Her Grace's woods and there were one or two other minor complaints, which I told Jackson I did not take seriously."

"Go on."

"I, however, received a letter from Jackson about two weeks ago, written laboriously, as I have said, he is not an articulate man, saying that there was consternation at one farm when not only some cattle went missing but one of their herdsmen had been beaten up and a girl of fifteen had disappeared."

The Marquis paused before he added,

"I realised then that this was definitely serious and I wrote to the Duchess stating what I had been told and asking for an explanation."

"And now you have her reply," Charlie said.

"Exactly," the Marquis answered "but it is not what I expected."

"Why not?"

"Because from what I had heard," the Marquis said, "and I must admit it is not much, she is an aggressive difficult woman who men like Jackson find it hard to express themselves to."

"What does she say in her letter?" Charlie enquired.

"She has written charmingly inviting me to stay with her tonight and saying that it would be easier to discuss the situation between our two estates than to allow our employees to come to loggerheads with each other."

The Marquis stared down at the letter as he went on,

"It sounds simple enough. At the same time it is not in keeping with what I have heard about her."

Charlie laughed.

"Now I will tell you what I know."

"That is what I want you to do," the Marquis nodded.

"The Duchess's father, the third Duke, was a friend of my father's," Charlie started. "He was a magnificent man, extremely good-looking, strong, fearless and a kind of hero of his age. He spent a great deal of his life travelling and there are stories about him which according to my grandfather and my father were told and re-told all over the world."

He laughed before he carried on,

"He was the sort of man who they said stopped a war single-handed, faced thousands of murderous tribesmen alone and performed other feats of skill and endurance that made the stories of him sound like something out of one of Scott's novels."

The Marquis was now extremely interested.

"Go on, Charlie. I had no idea of all this."

"It was long before our time," Charlie commented, "and Napoleon's War made us forget what happened in the last century."

"Go on telling me about the Duke."

"He was so busy with his heroic feats that according to my father women played little part in his life and he did not marry until just before he was forty."

"Very wise," the Marquis said dryly and his friend knew that at thirty-four the Marquis had said a dozen times that he had no intention of marrying if he could help it.

"Of course what the Duke wanted when he found that he had time to take a woman to the altar was what every man wants. A son."

The Marquis looked down at the letter he held in his hand and Charlie knew what he was thinking.

"That is what I am going to explain," he said. "His wife gave him a child the year after they were married, but it was a daughter."

"You mean to say that the Duchess of Grimstone is the late Duke's daughter?" the Marquis explained. "But how could she bear his title?"

"That is what I am going to tell you," Charlie answered. "He had carried out some very special service for the country, I cannot now remember what it was, and the King asked how he could reward him. He was already a Duke and there was no higher rank that he could attain. So the Duke requested that, if he did not produce a son before he died, the King should permit with the approval of Parliament, that the title be carried on in the female line as happens in Scotland."

"And the King agreed."

"Of course. It was a small reward for what the Duke had done. But what His Majesty did not know was that the Duke had already been told by the doctor that his wife could never have another child."

"That was bad luck," the Marquis remarked.

"Very bad where the Duke was concerned and, as it turned out for everybody else."

The way Charlie spoke made the Marquis look at him intently and he said,

"By the time the Duke's only child was grown up my father said that everybody was aware that she was strange and very different from other girls of her age."

"In what way?"

"She knew that, as she would be a Duchess and extremely wealthy, she was obviously a tremendous catch on the marriage market. So she decided to model herself on Queen Elizabeth."

The Marquis looked puzzled.

"What do you mean by that?"

"She encouraged her suitors. She played them off one against the other, but she made up her mind that no one but herself would ever control her fortune."

The Marquis smiled.

"In other words, she decided to become a 'Virgin Duchess'."

"Not exactly," Charlie replied. "Suitors for her hand came not only from the British Isles but from other countries that were not under the heel of Napoleon. Although she undoubtedly accepted some of them as lovers, she would not allow any of them to make an honest woman of her."

The Marquis laughed.

"She sounds amusing. I shall certainly accept her invitation!"

"It might have been amusing if as she grew older she had not developed into a tyrant. She has been described sometimes as a Circe or as a Medusa."

"What is she like now?" the Marquis enquired.

"I have not heard of her for some years," Charlie replied. "My father used to talk about her simply because he admired the old Duke. He said that power had gone to her head and she was that most frightening of creatures, a completely ruthless woman without a heart."

"Strong words," the Marquis said mockingly.

"The way my father talked made her seem to me to be somewhere between Lady Macbeth and the Queen of the Amazons."

The Marquis laughed again.

"After all you have said I shall most certainly accept the Duchess's invitation."

"I think it would be a mistake."

"A mistake?" the Marquis echoed. "Why?"

"Because some years ago when her beauty began to fade she withdrew from the Social world and lived exclusively down here at Grimstone House."

"That is why I suppose I have never heard about her," the Marquis commented.

"We did not have much chance during the War to hear about anybody!"

"That is true," the Marquis agreed. "At the same time what you have told me intrigues me."

"I thought it would," Charlie replied, "but I have lately heard rumours of some very unpleasant happenings that take place at Grimstone, which make me think that you would be wiser to stay away and express your complaints by letter rather than in person."

"You have already succeeded in making me more curious than I was before," the Marquis said, "so I shall look forward to meeting this Gorgon, if that is what she is."

"I am trying to remember all I have heard about her," Charlie continued, wrinkling his brow. "But you know what it is when you have not met the person being talked about. Everything goes in one ear and out of the other."

"You certainly do that with the things I tell you," the Marquis teased him.

"No, seriously," Charlie said, "from all I remember, she is shunned by all the decent people in this neighbourhood and there are tales, unless I am mistaken, of orgies at Grimstone House, which have shocked even those who took part in them."

"Who has been there whom we know?" the Marquis asked.

"I have a feeling, although I may be wrong, that Dagenham has been one of her guests."

"Good God! That old roué!" the Marquis exclaimed.

"Exactly. His reputation stinks, as you are well aware."

They were both thinking of a dissolute Peer who frequented the lowest and most unsavoury brothels in London, especially those that catered for 'exotic pleasures' that sickened any decent man.

The Marquis was staring down at the letter again and Charlie urged him,

"Do as I suggest, Mervyn, and write to the woman for explanations of what is going on. Do *not* accept her invitation."

"I am not as chicken-hearted as that," the Marquis said. "In fact everything you have told me makes me sure that the only sensible thing to do is to spy out the land for myself. What is more, if she is really as bad as you have painted her, I will not have her upsetting my tenants."

Charlie shrugged his shoulders.

"Be it on your own head," he said. "But if you have to spend an evening with Dagenham and the likes of him, don't blame me afterwards."

The Marquis walked to his desk.

"I will send a groom over right away to tell Her Grace that I will be with her at about six o'clock this afternoon. Don't go back to London, Charlie. Wait for me here and tomorrow I will regale you with my experiences, which I only hope are as dramatic as you suspect they will be."

The Marquis sat down at the desk as he spoke and, as he took a quill pen in his hand, he said,

"As I have no wish for you to be bored in my absence, you had better ask a few friends to dinner. The chef will get lazy if we don't give him enough to do."

"I will certainly give a dinner party," Charlie replied. "While you are drinking a bad claret, because no woman can choose a good wine, and conversing with Dagenham or watching some peculiar vice that will make your stomach turn, remember that I will be imbibing your best champagne."

The Marquis did not answer. He merely signed his name with a flourish and having read what he had written rang the silver bell that stood on his desk.

He handed the note to a footman who answered it telling him to send a groom immediately to Grimstone House.

As he spoke he thought, although he was not sure, there was a somewhat startled expression in the man's eyes.

Then he told himself that he was being imaginative and, as the door closed, he said to Charlie,

"By the way, how old is the Duchess now?"

"She must be getting on a bit," Charlie answered, "forty-five or more, but still, I expect, playing 'hard to get'. There are always fortune-hunters, whatever a woman's age, if she is rich enough."

"I have always known you to be truthful, at least to me," the Marquis said, "but I think your whole tale is a lot of moonshine. The thing however that astonishes me is that not only you speak of her as if she was a Dragon incarnate, but so does Jackson."

Charlie laughed.

"It will certainly be an anti-climax if she turns out to be a quiet little woman with greying hair who has taken to knitting. After all it can hardly be her fault that a girl of fifteen has disappeared."

"Bad Masters make bad servants," the Marquis said quietly, "and what Jackson tells me makes me think that she has become a bogey who frightens everyone on my estate."

"Well, set off on your voyage of discovery and I will certainly keep the house warm until you return. Meanwhile, may I write notes to the friends I intend to invite here this evening?"

"Of course," the Marquis agreed, "and I presume it will be an all-male party?"

"If I had known that you were going to leave me like this," Charlie replied, "I might have brought a pretty Cyprian down with me from London. I cannot believe that there is much to choose from in Newmarket."

"Most of the women I have seen so far," the Marquis said dryly, "would make quite good-looking horses!"

Charlie laughed.

"They always say one grows like one's pets, but for a woman to look like a horse is a disaster!"

"From your description of the Duchess she should look like a snake."

"Any sort of monster will do," Charlie laughed, "but remember she was, according to reports, very beautiful when she was young."

"I must polish up my compliments," the Marquis smiled, "and seriously, Charlie, I believe in living amicably with one's neighbours. A feud between two neighbouring landlords is, I am certain, a great mistake."

"Of course it is," Charlie agreed. "That is the sort of thing my father thought."

He paused before he added mischievously,

"You know, Mervyn, I am beginning to think you are ageing rather rapidly. I shall miss the daredevil Officer who was always prepared to crawl round the enemy's defences and take him by surprise."

"The way you are speaking makes it sound extremely foolhardy," the Marquis remarked, "but if you remember, we discussed every move, planned every step and the reason why we were successful when we captured those guns was that we had left nothing to chance."

"You are right," Charlie agreed, "but what you are doing now is walking straight into the enemy's hands and I have a feeling, although I may be wrong, that you will find it a hornet's nest."

"If it is, I shall withdraw in the face of superior odds!" the Marquis shrugged his shoulders.

*

The Reverend Theophilus Stanton rose from the breakfast table and, closing carefully the book he had been reading so as not to lose his place, walked towards the door.

As he reached it, his niece called after him,

"Uncle Theophilus, you have forgotten to open your letter."

"It's sure to be a bill," her uncle replied, "but I have not the time nor the money for it at the moment."

He left the room closing the door behind him and Aspasia looked across the table at her twin brother and laughed.

"That is just like Uncle Theophilus. He always avoids unpleasantness, if he possibly can."

"He is very wise," Jerome Stanton replied.

He was always called 'Jerry' by everybody who knew him and was an extremely good-looking young man, tall broad-shouldered with fair hair and blue eyes.

He had a broad forehead, which not only denoted brains but also gave him a frank and open look that made people he met like and trust him.

"You are as irresponsible as he is!" Aspasia teased.

Although they were twins, she was very unlike her brother. She was small, slim and very lovely, but instead of fair hair, hers had a touch of fire in it that made it almost red and her eyes were a far darker blue so that looking at them together it would have been difficult to guess they had been born at the same time.

"Will you have some more coffee?" she asked.

"No, thank you," her brother replied. "But you had better open Uncle's letter and learn the worst. I hope it is not for a very large amount."

His sister looked at him sharply.

"You are not hard up again, Jerry?"

"Of course I am," he replied. "You have no idea how expensive Oxford University is."

"You knew when you went there that you would have to economise in every way because the money Mama had left us has almost run out."

"I know! I know," Jerry exclaimed. "But it is difficult when I am with a lot of fellows who are richer than I am to keep accepting hospitality without giving any."

Aspasia was silent.

Then their uncle who they lived with had only a very small stipend and, as she had just said to her brother, the money that her mother had left them when she died five years ago had been spent over the years on their education until there was practically nothing left in the Bank.

As Jerry knew the position as well as she did, there was no point in saying anything more and Aspasia reached out her hand towards the letter and picked it up.

To her surprise it did not look like a bill and was written on a thick white parchment that was so expensive that Aspasia stared at it before she turned it over.

Then she gave a little cry of sheer astonishment.

"What is it?" Jerry asked her at once.

"This letter is from the Duchess," she said. "Look! Here is her coronet on the back."

Brother and sister looked at each other meaningfully before Aspasia said in a frightened voice almost beneath her breath,

"Why should she be – writing to – Uncle Theophilus?"

"Open it and find out," Jerry proposed. "It is a good thing, if you ask me, that he did not notice who the letter was from. It would have upset him."

"Yes, of course," Aspasia agreed.

For a moment she sat staring at the letter as if she could not force herself to learn its contents.

Then meaningfully with a silver butter knife she slit open the top of the envelope.

As she drew out the thick sheet of paper inside, she felt perceptively that it was bad news and it was almost as if there was a vibration of evil coming from the paper itself.

She did not speak, but she was aware that Jerry was watching her as she opened the letter.

She read what was written without speaking until Jerry was unable to contain his curiosity any longer and demanded,

"What does it say? Read it to me."

"I cannot believe it! It cannot be true," Aspasia cried.

"What does it say?" Jerry asked again.

Aspasia drew in her breath and in a voice that trembled she read,

"To the Reverend Theophilus Stanton.

On the instructions of Her Grace the Duchess of Grimstone, now that you have reached the age of sixty-five, you are retired from your Living and you will vacate the Vicarage within a month of this date.

Yours faithfully,
Erasmus Carstairs,
Secretary to Her Grace."

As Aspasia finished reading, her voice broke and her eyes were filled with tears, while Jerry brought his fist down violently on the table so that the plates and cups rattled.

"*Curse her!*" he exclaimed. "How can she do a thing like this to Uncle Theophilus? It's inhumane! Brutal!"

"How can he leave here?" Aspasia asked. "The people in the village love him and he loves them. Besides, where can we go?"

She stared across the table at her twin as she asked the question, seeing her brother through her tears and knowing that he was as perturbed as she was.

"Uncle Theophilus has been here all his life," Jerry pointed out as if he spoke to himself. "Just as we have."

They were both thinking that the Vicarage was so much their home that they had never thought of it as belonging to anybody else.

Grimstone House, the Duchess's ancestral home was five miles away, but it might to all intents and purposes have been in another world.

Here in Little Medlock life was slow and easy. The villagers came to Church because they wished to worship God and they brought their troubles and their joys to the Vicar because he belonged to them. What happened on other parts of the estate did not concern them.

"How can we tell Uncle Theophilus?" Aspasia asked her brother.

"It will not be easy," Jerry said, "and you realise this means that I will not be able to go back to Oxford?"

Aspasia gave a little cry.

"Why not?"

Then even as she spoke she knew the answer.

If the little money they had, and it was indeed little enough, had to be spent in finding somewhere else to live, they both knew that it was very unlikely that at sixty-five the Reverend Theophilus would be given another Living.

Of course he could apply to the Bishop but, even if another Parish was found for him, it would still break his heart to leave his flock who he looked upon as his children and to whom he was certainly their Pastor and shepherd.

Aspasia looked down at the letter again.

'This was not written by the Duchess," she said, "but by her secretary."

"She instructed him to write it," Jerry answered.

Aspasia looked at her brother.

"You don't think that she suspects in any way?"

"Why should she?" Jerry asked.

But there had been a pause before he answered and a flicker in his eyes that his sister did not miss.

"Martha was saying a few days ago that people in the village had remarked on your likeness to a certain person whose name we do not mention."

"It is nothing that I am ashamed of," Jerry said defiantly.

"No, of course not, dearest," Aspasia agreed, "but we are both well aware that it is dangerous."

She paused for a moment before she went on,

"Perhaps it would be wise for us to go away. I am always afraid from all the things we hear about her that somebody will make her suspicious about you."

"Why should anybody do that?"

"I was looking at the miniature Mama had of him and you are very very like him, the same forehead, the same eyes and the same coloured hair! And, of course, you are tall as he was and everybody always says how magnificent he was."

Jerry looked over his shoulder almost as if he thought that somebody might be listening.

"It is wisest not to talk about him, we both know that."

"It is wrong, I know," Aspasia said, "but just lately I have been feeling afraid."

"Why particularly lately?"

Aspasia gave her brother a smile that seemed to illuminate her face.

"Because, Jerry, dearest, you grow more handsome and more attractive every time I see you. You have grown up in the last year and that is when you have become so like him."

"As a matter of fact, Aspasia," Jerry said, "one or two of the older people at Oxford have said that I reminded them of somebody, but they could not think who it was and it puzzled them."

"Oh, Jerry, you must be careful and that is why I think perhaps it is a good idea – for us to go away."

"Where could we go? You know we have no money."

Aspasia looked down again at the letter in her hands.

Then the door opened and instinctively, as if she had not made up her mind what to do about it, she put it quickly in her lap under the table.

But it was not her uncle who came into the room as she had expected, but Martha, the maid who had been with her mother and who had looked after the twins ever since they were born.

"Oh, Miss Aspasia," she cried, "I've had bad news!"

Jerry jumped to his feet.

"What is it, Martha? What has happened?" he asked.

Martha put her hands up to her eyes and sat down in the nearest chair.

"It's knocked me right over," she said, "comin' so early in the mornin'."

"What has?" Aspasia enquired.

"It's Flo, my sister Flo. She's – dead!"

As she said the word, Martha's voice broke and she sobbed into her handkerchief.

Then determinedly she blew her nose sharply and wiped her eyes and said,

"It was to be expected, but it's just the shock that has got me for the moment. I'll ask your uncle if he'll drive me over in his gig and perform the Burial Service."

"When did she die?" Aspasia asked her.

She knew all about Martha's sister Flo, who had been ailing for years and was always on the point of death, and yet invariably revived just when they had made up their minds that nothing could save her.

"Three days ago," Martha replied, "and you'd think they'd have let me know afore now."

She sniffed indignantly as she added,

"I daresay as they wouldn't have told me at all if it hadn't been that they wanted the Reverend. They couldn't bury her without him."

"I will go and tell Uncle Theophilus that you want to go over to Greater Medlock at once," Aspasia said, "and Jerry will put Bessy in the gig while you are putting on your cloak and bonnet."

As Aspasia spoke, she slipped the letter from her lap under the tea tray in front of her and rose to walk to Martha's side and put her arm around her shoulder.

She bent and kissed her cheek saying as she did so,

"I am sorry, Martha. It must be a great shock to you. I know how kind and loving you always were to Flo."

She could not help thinking as she spoke that it was a merciful release.

Flo had been the whining sort and Martha, although always busy, would often walk the three miles to Greater Medlock and back again just to listen to her sister's complaints, which half the time were imaginary.

"There be some cold meat for your luncheon, Miss Aspasia," Martha said in her usual crisp tone as she rose to her feet, "and I've got the salad ready. If you put the potatoes in the oven in about two hours' time, they'll be nice and hot when you and Master Jerry wants them."

"Don't worry about us," Aspasia said, "and I will pick some flowers from the garden for your sister's grave."

"That's ever so kind of you," Martha replied. "And don't worry about the breakfast things. I'll wash them up when I comes back."

She hurried away as she spoke, her momentary weakness gone, ready now to take charge of the situation as she had done at every crisis that had arisen ever since the twins could remember.

It was only when Aspasia and Jerry had seen their uncle drive off in his gig with Martha beside him that Aspasia remembered the letter on the breakfast table.

As she and Jerry went back into the house, she said,

"I have an idea!"

"What is it?" he asked.

"I am going to see the Duchess and ask her to reconsider her decision."

"You are going to do nothing of the sort!" her brother answered, his voice rising.

"There is just a chance, just a chance that she might be kind and understanding if she learns just how much Uncle Theophilus means – to the people in the village."

"Kind?" Jerry asked. "You must be raving! We know what she is like. What about Albert Newlands?"

Aspasia shrugged her shoulders.

"We don't know the Duchess did that."

"But there was no doubt that it was done on her instructions."

"How do we know? Bollard would say so, of course he would, but she may have no idea of the things he has done and I just don't believe that any woman could be so cruel."

"I forbid you to go and see her," Jerry insisted.

"What have we to lose?" Aspasia said. "Uncle Theophilus has been told that he has to go, which means that we have to find somewhere else to live and you will have to leave Oxford. In fact, if you do not find work of some sort, we shall doubtless starve. I personally prefer to go down on my knees and beg for mercy."

"If you do, she will doubtless kick you."

"We have heard all these stories about her ever since we have been children," Aspasia said. "We have never seen her and you know as well as I do how village people exaggerate because they have nothing else to talk about."

"I have heard a lot of things that you have not," Jerry said.

"What sort of things?"

"About the parties she holds up at the house."

"I have heard of those too and you know the people in this village think that any party where there is drinking and dancing is a feast of Satan. They are still very primitive in this part of the world. Because most of them cannot read they have to rely on gossip which they exaggerate and exaggerate as storytellers have done since the beginning of the world."

Jerry laughed.

"You are very convincing, Aspasia, but I still cannot allow you to go."

"One thing is very certain," Aspasia said. "You cannot go yourself."

"No, of course not."

"But you will leave us to be thrown out into the street without a penny, without making some sort of protest?"

Her brother walked restlessly across the room.

"I am sure that Grimstone House is not the place for you."

"How do you know? You have never been there."

"No, of course not. But the things I have heard – "

"The things you have heard!" Aspasia mocked him. "The people here in Little Medlock have blown the Duchess up into a kind of female devil just because they have nothing else to talk about. If she does hold Bacchanalian orgies I wonder who takes part in them? There are few people living around here who would know what it was even if they saw one."

It was true, Jerry admitted to himself, that they had very few neighbours.

When he and Aspasia rode together on the horses they broke in themselves and which were their only means of transport they often journeyed for two or three hours without seeing a soul.

They kept well away from Grimstone House and the part of the estate that was cultivated and farmed by the Duchess. But there were the woods and the wide-open country where there was only bracken and gorse bushes with no sign of human habitation and they might, as Aspasia had often said, have been riding on the moon.

"I don't like it," Jerry said now. "I am sure it is wrong and that I should stop you from going."

"I *am* going!" Aspasia said firmly. "If she says no, well, we shall be no worse off than we are now, but I might be able in some way to change her mind. After all she is a woman. She must realise that an elderly man like Uncle Theophilus would find it impossible to start a new life somewhere else."

She saw the expression on her brother's face and added,

"I am aware, dearest, what it would mean to you to leave Oxford and you know that above all things Mama wanted us to have a good education. She said so a hundred times and when she was dying she said to me,

"'You and Jerry must be properly educated, darling, so that if you use your intelligence, I am sure that however difficult it may seem now you will find a place in the world where you will both be very happy.'"

"A place in the world," Jerry repeated beneath his breath. "It would be easier to find something to do if I had a Degree."

"You have to go back to Oxford." Aspasia said. "You have to! And nobody and nothing shall stop you. I *will* make the Duchess see sense."

She spoke almost as if she was inspired as she went on,

"We have always believed in what is right and good and I am sure now that God will help us and you will one day have everything that is yours by right."

"You are daydreaming!" Jerry declared.

"No, I am saying what is in my heart and in my mind," Aspasia cried, "and more than that, it is almost as if I am being directed, perhaps by Mama. The first step is to go to Grimstone House and nothing you can say or do will stop me."

"Very well," Jerry agreed, "but you know as well as I do that I dare not be seen anywhere near the house."

"No, of course not," Aspasia replied. "We will ride our usual way East of the woods until we are parallel with the house and then I will go on alone. You don't need to wait. I will find my own way home."

"I would much rather wait for you."

"That might be unwise if you are seen hanging about. And apart from that, supposing she thinks it wrong for a lady to ride without a groom and sends one with me?"

"I am sure that is very unlikely."

"I am only pointing out the possibility."

"Very well," Jerry conceded. "I will leave you as near to the house as is safe, then I will come back here and kick my heels until you appear. But make no mistake, I will be extremely anxious and worried as to what is happening."

"I will not be exactly looking forward to it," Aspasia said in a small voice, "but I know in my heart that it is something I have to do if only to prove to myself that I have tried my best to save Uncle Theophilus."

"And me," Jerry murmured.

CHAPTER TWO

When Aspasia had left Jerry and was riding through the woods alone she began to feel nervous.

Because she was so determined to get her own way and try to persuade the Duchess to be merciful, she had not told her brother of her fears and had tried to keep him from realising that she was in fact very frightened.

However, because as twins they were so closely attuned to each other, Jerry, although he was not in other respects very perceptive, said when they had pulled their horses to a standstill outside the wood,

"Change your mind, dearest. I know it is a mistake for you to walk into the lion's den. We will manage somehow."

"On what?" Aspasia enquired.

There was silence and she knew that even Jerry, who was always carefree and optimistic, was thinking how very little money they had left and that without their uncle's stipend it would be impossible for them to live without some other source of income.

"All right, have it your own way," he accepted, "but promise me that when you have talked to the Duchess you will come home immediately."

"I certainly will," Aspasia promised, "but don't wait. As I have already said, she might decide to send a groom with me."

"I will go back to the Vicarage and wait. But you know that I will be worrying about you."

"I doubt it," Aspasia smiled. "I have never known you worry about anything particularly."

They both laughed.

Aspasia had spoken the truth when she said that Jerry never worried. It was because he took life as it came and made the best of whatever situation he found himself in.

It was a gift that she wished she had herself, for like her mother she worried about many things, especially lately, wondering what the future would be when the money that they had been living on and which had paid so far for Jerry to go to Oxford came to an end.

At any other time Aspasia knew that she would have enjoyed riding through unfamiliar woods and knowing that the sun shining through the fir trees making a pattern of gold on the mossy ground was very beautiful.

She followed a small twisting path that wound between the trees until suddenly the wood came to an end and in front of her was Grimstone House.

She had never seen it before. Although the descriptions that other people had made her of it had given her some idea of what it was like, it was far more magnificent and far more imposing than she had expected.

It was very old, having been built by the family long before they were made Dukes and added to by every succeeding generation.

Standing on high ground with green parkland in front of it where there were herds of spotted deer it looked to Aspasia like something out of one of her dreams.

Slowly she rode on, thinking that it would be impossible for anybody to be really bad or wicked if they lived in such beautiful surroundings and trying to convince herself that the stories she had heard about the Duchess were baseless.

As she had said to Jerry, she was sure that the cruel actions that were carried out in the Duchess's name on the estate were performed without her knowledge and that her Agent, a man called Bollard, was entirely responsible for them.

She reached the main drive that cut through the Park and led directly to the house and, as she rode on, Aspasia felt her heart beating in a frightened manner. She knew only too well that Jerry's future depended on the outcome of this visit to the Duchess.

'Perhaps she will not see me,' she mused nervously.

Then, because there was nothing else that she could do, she began to pray to God, as she believed her uncle would pray if he knew what she was doing.

Then she spoke to her mother,

'Help me, Mama! *Help me*!' she breathed in the depths of her heart. 'Wherever you are I know that you will still be loving Jerry and me and at this moment we need your help desperately.'

She was still praying when she reached the front door.

There were a number of grey stone steps leading up to it and she sat for a moment looking round a little helplessly, wondering how she could leave her horse and reach the door.

Just then a groom came running from the side of the house and, as he went to her horse's head, she smiled at him and said,

"Thank you, but will you wait a moment before you take my horse to the stables? I have no appointment and perhaps Her Grace will be unable to see me."

The groom was young, but he looked at Aspasia with admiration as he touched his forehead and replied,

"I'll wait, ma'am."

She slipped from the saddle onto the ground and walked up the steps, but before she could look for a bell or raise the knocker the door opened.

At the first glance she saw that there were three footmen in attendance in a Great Hall with a marble floor, Ionic pillars and exquisitely executed paintings on the walls.

Aspasia walked forward another step and was just wondering whether she should speak to the footmen when an elderly butler appeared and came towards her.

"Good morning, madam," he greeted her in a respectful tone that also implied a question.

"If it is possible," Aspasia said in a voice that she felt was commendably calm, "I wish to see Her Grace – the Duchess."

"Her Grace is not expecting you, madam?"

"No, but would you please inform Her Grace that – it is of the utmost importance."

"If you will come this way, madam," the butler suggested, "I will enquire if Her Grace is available."

He walked ahead of Aspasia who followed him through the Great Hall until he opened a door and she was shown into what she thought must be an anteroom.

It seemed large and impressive to her, but she guessed that the main rooms in the house would be larger still.

"May I enquire your name, madam?" the butler asked politely.

"Miss Aspasia Stanton."

The man bowed and left the room and Aspasia stood looking around her.

She had never seen such impressive furnishings or such magnificent pictures before and she stared at them with interest recognising many of the artists from the lessons that her mother had arranged for her to have on art, a subject that she told Aspasia every educated person should be knowledgeable about.

"Although I shall never see such beautiful pictures myself," Aspasia had said once, "at least I can dream about them and imagine what they look like."

"Nobody can prevent us from dreaming," her mother had replied.

But while her lips had smiled there had been an inexpressible pain in her eyes that Aspasia understood.

As she looked eagerly about her, she realised she must tell Jerry that she had actually seen a Rubens.

Then on the other side of the room she saw a Poussin and wondered how she could explain to him how beautiful it was and how impossible to imagine unless one actually saw it.

She had time to look at only two more pictures before the door opened and the butler came back into the room.

For the moment Aspasia felt that her heart had stopped beating.

If he reported that the Duchess would not see her, there was nothing she could do but go away.

"Will you come this way, madam?" he said. "Her Grace will give you a few minutes of her time, but you will appreciate that you are very fortunate to be given an audience at such short notice."

"Yes, indeed, and I am – very grateful," Aspasia said humbly.

She had the feeling that the butler was repeating what he had been told to say, but she was too grateful to be in any way critical.

At least she had a chance of putting her case in front of the Duchess and she must concentrate on her uncle and what it would mean to him to be turned away from his beloved Parish.

The butler led the way down a broad corridor where again there were a number of pictures that Aspasia longed to look at and beneath them five pieces of furniture, some of which she was sure were French and had been made in the Louis XIV period.

Another door lay ahead of them and outside stood two footmen on duty. As they threw open the door, the butler announced in a voice that sounded like a fanfare of trumpets,

"Miss Aspasia Stanton, Your Grace."

For a moment because she was nervous everything seemed to swim in front of Aspasia's eyes.

Then she saw that she was in a large room with the sunshine coming in through diamond-paned windows that reached high up the walls.

It flashed through her mind that this must be a very old part of the house.

Then she could think of nothing but the woman she had come to see.

The Duchess was standing in front of an ornately carved fireplace and she was taller than Aspasia had expected and very much more impressive.

Dressed in the latest fashion, which was very much more elaborate than anything that had reached Little Medlock, she was wearing several strings of huge pearls, diamonds in her ears and around her wrists and a number of rings on her long thin fingers.

It was then that Aspasia looked at her face and found it impossible to look away.

Never had she imagined that any woman could look so beautiful and at the same time so evil.

She could not explain to herself exactly why she knew that the woman facing her was as wicked as she was reputed to be.

But the vibrations that came from her were so positive that Aspasia felt something within herself recoil as if they had struck her physically.

Then, as she moved slowly towards the Duchess, she could not help admitting that, though in some way she looked old, she was still beautiful.

Her hair might once have been fair, but now it was dyed red, an artificial red, but still a compellingly attractive colour that made her skin look very white.

Her features were almost perfectly classical, her eyes, which were naturally large, had mascaraed eyelashes and her eyelids were coloured green.

The whole effect was fantastic yet compelling and Aspasia's eyes were still on the Duchess's face as she drew near and yet nearer.

"You wanted to see me?" the Duchess asked sharply and her voice was hard.

Belatedly Aspasia, because she was so bemused, remembered to curtsey.

"I am very grateful to Your Grace," she began, "for – allowing me to – do so."

Her voice trembled, but when she rose she held her head high and her chin went up.

'I must not be frightened,' she thought. 'There is too much at stake.'

"Who are you and what do you want?"

"I am the niece, Your Grace, of the Reverend Theophilus Stanton – who has received a letter from Your Grace's secretary telling him that because he is now sixty-five – he must leave his Parish of Little Medlock."

"Yes, that is right," the Duchess replied. "I have no use for old people on the estate. I am getting rid of them all. I want young people around me with ideas.

People with vitality. Old age is a disease and it is infectious!"

Aspasia felt that she could not have heard aright.

And then she said,

"I thought Your Grace might not be aware how loved my uncle is in Little Medlock and – how much he has done for the people there. He would find it difficult to find another Living and not only will he be lost without his parishioners – but they will be lost and unhappy without him."

Aspasia's voice was very soft and pleading.

"I am not interested in what the people of Little Medlock feel or do not feel," the Duchess retorted harshly. "They will do as I tell them. Your uncle is too old and I will find a young man to replace him."

Aspasia gave a little cry.

"Please – please – Your Grace – " she started to plead.

Quite suddenly there was an interruption.

The door opened and a woman came hurrying into the room.

She looked, Aspasia thought, liked a superior servant.

She was plainly dressed and yet the way she walked towards the Duchess and the way she spoke seemed to have a certain authority about her that seemed out of place in someone in a subservient position.

She reached the Duchess's side and spoke in a low voice as if she did not wish Aspasia to hear what was said and yet every word was quite audible.

"It's no use, Your Grace. She's running a high temperature and there's no chance of her coming down for dinner this evening."

"Damn the little fool! This is a nice time to be ill!" the Duchess blurted out furiously.

Aspasia was astonished.

She had never thought is possible that a lady of the Duchess's standing would swear.

"There's nothing I can do, Your Grace," the woman went on. "If I got her on her feet, she'd be worse than useless in the state she's in."

"Then what the devil are we to do?" the Duchess asked. "We cannot switch any of the other girls. You know as well as I do Lord Dagenham always expects to have Gracie and Lord Wilbraham will not look at anybody but Nina."

"I know, I know!" the woman replied, "but there's no time to bring another girl down from London."

"I suppose Louise might do at a pinch."

"Oh, no, Your Grace. Louise is all right for the unsophisticated, a young boy who needs encouraging, but with an experienced man she's far too blatant."

"I told you that this evening was important," the Duchess said angrily, "and if there is one thing that makes me lose my temper it is when my plans go wrong."

"I know, Your Grace, but no one can prevent illness and I assure you the girl's really ill."

"She will be even more ill by the time I have finished with her!" the Duchess growled.

She spoke in such a sinister way that Aspasia shuddered and the slight movement she made attracted the Duchess's attention.

She turned to look at her and she said in a voice still reverberating with anger,

"As for you – you can go back and tell – "

Suddenly she stopped and it seemed to Aspasia that her eyes narrowed, her green lids giving her almost the expression of a tiger.

Aspasia thought that she had failed miserably in her mission. Jerry had been right. It had been quite hopeless coming here and she had been foolish to expect mercy from a woman who would swear or talk in such a violent and unpleasant manner.

She told herself that at least she would go with dignity, thank the Duchess for receiving her, curtsey and leave the room.

"Take off your bonnet!"

It was an order and Aspasia looked bewildered.

"You heard what I said," the Duchess said when she did not move. "Take off your bonnet so that we can see your hair."

Thinking that this was as surprising as everything else that had happened since she came to the house, Aspasia undid the blue ribbons of the plain bonnet she wore.

Because she was calling on the Duchess she had not put on her riding habit to go to Grimstone House, but instead had worn the pretty gown she wore on Sundays which had a full skirt and a small tight-fitting jacket over it.

Her clothes were always made by Martha, who was very skilful with her needle, and she would have been horrified if she had known that Aspasia was riding in one of the few decent gowns she had to wear on other occasions.

She had, however, wished to look her best at her interview with the Duchess, although now she had seen her and the house she realised that nothing she possessed would look anything but inadequate in such surroundings.

She pulled off her bonnet and the sun from the window caught the fiery gold in her hair and made it look as if there were little flames dancing on her head.

Aspasia tried to smooth it neatly into shape and, as she raised her dark-blue eyes, she saw that both the other women were staring at her strangely in a manner that she did not understand.

"You say you are staying with your uncle," the Duchess asked. "Where are your parents?"

"My father and mother are – both dead."

The Duchess glanced at the woman standing next to her and it seemed as if they communicated without words.

There was silence and then the Duchess said slowly,

"You came here to petition me on behalf of your uncle. To beg that he should be allowed to stay in his Living?"

"That is right – Your Grace."

There was just a flicker of hope in Aspasia's heart. She did not understand what was happening, but she sensed that the atmosphere had changed.

The Duchess was no longer angry and she felt that perhaps at the eleventh hour Uncle Theophilus might be saved.

"I have a proposition to put to you," the Duchess now said. "If you will stay here for the night and do exactly what you are told without arguing and without complaining, then I will agree that your uncle may stay where he is."

Aspasia gave a gasp and the room seemed suddenly to be filled with sunshine.

"Do you really mean that – Your Grace? Of course I will stay. I will do – anything you ask of me if Uncle Theophilus may remain at – Little Medlock."

"He may," the Duchess agreed, "but you must swear to me on everything you hold sacred that you will do exactly what you are told to do."

"I – swear," Aspasia said.

The Duchess looked at the woman standing next to her.

"You have not long to instruct her."

She was again speaking in a low voice which Aspasia felt that there was no reason for since she could easily hear what was said.

"I'll manage, Your Grace."

"She is to wear the snowdrop gown," the Duchess ordered. "It always works with the more sophisticated ones."

The other woman gave her a smile.

"You leave it to me, Your Grace. I've never failed you yet."

"Nor has my luck," the Duchess replied. "Who would have thought that the Vicar of Little Medlock would come to my rescue?"

She laughed, but Aspasia felt that it was not a particularly pleasant sound. At the same time she was too happy to be critical.

She had won! She had won!

The only thing that worried her was what Jerry would think when she did not return home as he expected.

"Now you come along with me," the woman was saying.

Aspasia, however, remembered her manners.

"Thank you, Your Grace, more than I can possibly say," she said. "I am very very grateful to you – as I know my uncle will be and all the people in the village."

"Well, show your gratitude by doing what you are told," the Duchess replied.

Then, as she looked at Aspasia, the expression on her face seemed to change and, although it was difficult to explain even to herself, Aspasia realised that in some way the Duchess was hating her.

For a moment she was surprised and then almost as if she had been told the reason she knew that it was because she was young and the Duchess was old.

Once again feeling frightened she curtseyed and hurried after the other woman who had almost reached the door.

As they left the salon for the corridor, the woman said,

"We've a lot to do so I suggest if you're hungry you'd better eat first and then let's get to work."

Aspasia looked at her as if for explanation and she said,

"You'll find out what it is as we go along. But I hope if you've been nicely brought up you'll know how to handle your knives and forks and how to behave at the table without my having to teach you that."

Aspasia looked at her in sheer astonishment before she exclaimed,

"I should hope so!"

The woman laughed.

"You'd be surprised how ignorant most girls are when they've never been in a place like this before."

"Nor have I," Aspasia admitted, "and it is very beautiful and very magnificent. When there is time I would love to look at the pictures."

"Pictures? You won't have time for them."

They reached the hall and went towards the stairs.

As they did so Aspasia said,

"My horse was taken to the stables. Perhaps I ought to say that I shall not be wanting him – until tomorrow morning."

"Yes, of course," the woman agreed.

As she spoke, Aspasia had another idea.

"I wonder," she said hesitatingly, "if it would be possible for a groom – to take a message to the

Vicarage to say that – I shall be staying here tonight. My uncle will be worried if I do not return."

She knew as she spoke that it would not be her uncle who would be worried but Jerry, but that was something she could not mention.

"Yes, I am sure that can be arranged," the woman said.

She turned to the butler.

"Mr. Newlands will you see that Miss Stanton's horse is taken back to the Vicarage and tell them that she will not be returning until tomorrow morning. We'll send her home in one of our carriages."

"Yes, of course, Mrs. Fielding," the butler replied. "I'll see to it."

"Thank you," Aspasia said. "Thank you very much."

Mrs. Fielding started to climb the stairs and Aspasia followed her.

She was thinking as she did so that she had to let Jerry know that she would not be coming back, otherwise in his usual impulsive manner he might come in search of her and that would be disastrous.

'By the time the grooms reach the Vicarage Martha will be back and will open the door,' she told herself.

Nevertheless she was worrying as she walked on up the stairs and along a corridor that seemed interminable. But whatever difficulties there might be about her staying, the only thing that really mattered was that Uncle Theophilus was saved and so was Jerry.

He could now return to Oxford and her prayers had been answered.

'Thank you, Mama, thank you,' she said in her heart.

*

The Marquis rode towards Grimstone House and he thought as Aspasia had that it was certainly more impressive than he had expected.

He had sent his valet ahead in a brake that contained his luggage and rode not only because he preferred riding and needed the exercise but also because he wanted to try out one of the latest acquisitions to his stable.

This was an exceedingly fine stallion that was obstreperous enough to keep his Master interested in controlling him and had a speed that the Marquis appreciated was exceptional.

He had bought the horse recently at a sale and knew the moment he saw it led into the ring that it was an animal that he must acquire whatever the price.

It carried him from Newmarket to Grimstone House in what the Marquis was sure was a record time and he was therefore in a very good humour when he pulled the stallion to a standstill outside the front door.

Because he was expected, a groom was waiting together with several other grooms, which told the Marquis that he would not be the only visitor.

He stepped in through the front door, handed his tall hat, gloves and whip to one of the footmen and the butler led him to a room that was obviously one of the State salons and as impressive as the house itself.

Although it was still early in the evening, the candles in the huge crystal chandeliers were lit and they glittered on the Duchess as she advanced towards him.

As the Marquis looked at her, he thought, as Aspasia had done, that he had never seen a more sensational or extraordinary woman.

Charlie had certainly not exaggerated when he said that she had been beautiful, but the Marquis realised that at forty-five no artifice, however skilfully applied, could disguise the fact that she was growing old.

Her figure, however, was thin and lissom. He fancied that there was something serpent-like about her, while he found that her hand as she held it out with an affected eagerness was cold when he touched it.

"My Lord, I am so delighted that you should have accepted my invitation."

"It is exceedingly kind of Your Grace to invite me," the Marquis replied.

Her eyes with their green lids seemed to glint at him from under her darkened eyelashes.

"Business is so boring unless we contrive to make it more amusing," she said in a low seductive voice, "and that is what I hope we shall be able to do this evening."

"I hope so too," the Marquis replied.

A servant appeared at his elbow with a glass of champagne and, as the Marquis sipped it,m he was aware that Charlie had been wrong in claiming that a woman could not choose wine. The champagne was exceptionally good.

'At least,' he told himself, 'the evening is starting well.'

"I have a party tonight," the Duchess was saying, "but some of my guests have not yet arrived. However I would like you to meet those who have."

The Duchess then introduced him to two gentlemen, each with high-sounding foreign titles and a rather vacant-looking Peer who the Marquis vaguely remembered having heard was making a fool of himself in London by gambling for astronomical stakes.

The Duchess, however, had no intention of boring him with people he did not know.

She led the Marquis across the room to a sofa where they were out of earshot of the others and she then started to flatter him in a manner that he realised was subtle and at the same time intelligent.

The Duchess obviously knew more about him than he did about her and he found her amusing and she made him laugh.

Finally, when they had conversed without referring in any way to the reason for his coming to Grimstone House, she suggested,

"As you have quite a long evening's entertainment in front of you, I feel sure you would like to be shown your room. You will not wish to hurry over dressing."

The Marquis agreed. He had no wish to take the initiative in what he either did or said until he could see how the land lay and make his own judgement as to what was to be expected.

For the moment he certainly found the Duchess unusual and he could understand that her appearance, if nothing else, would scandalise any neighbours she might have.

Where a woman was concerned, it was always to be expected that people would gossip and complain if for no other reason because they were jealous.

At the same time he had not forgotten the things that Jackson had told him and he thought that he would be careful at dinner not to allow the wine, if it was as good as the champagne he was now drinking, to influence him.

He was shown upstairs to what he was sure was one of the finest rooms in the house and he recognised that the Duchess was determined to impress him.

He wondered if his letter asking for an explanation of the troubles on their boundaries had perturbed her. If it had, all the better.

As he had said to Charlie, it was a great mistake for adjoining owners to quarrel with each other and the sooner the difficulties between them were cleared up the better.

The Marquis's valet, Jenkins, who had been with him for many years and had also been his batman in the Army, had already unpacked and was waiting for him.

As the Marquis took off his riding coat, he said,

"Well, Jenkins, what do you think of this place?"

"I don't like it, my Lord."

"Not like it? Why not?"

"There's somethin' goin' on here, my Lord, as ain't right."

The Marquis looked at him in astonishment.

"Now why should you think that, Jenkins?"

He knew as he spoke that he wanted to hear his valet's opinion.

Jenkins had a sharp common sense that he had found advantageous not only in war but also in peace.

He was not a scandalmonger, but what he ferreted out in his own way was usually accurate and the Marquis was well aware that he could always rely on Jenkins to tell him the truth.

"It's nothin' I can put me finger on right away, my Lord," Jenkins replied, "but I'll get to the bottom of it before we leave, you can rely on that."

"I am relying on you, as I always do, Jenkins."

The Marquis knew that Jenkins would have learned when they were at Newmarket some of the information that Jackson had related to him and he was sure that when they came here that the valet would be curious to see if such stories were true.

The Marquis found that a bath had been prepared for him in a powder room that had been converted from its original use.

As he stepped into the warm water, which was at exactly the right temperature, he said,

"At least we are provided with every comfort. Who else is staying in the house?"

"They wouldn't tell me that, my Lord, but I think, if you asks me, you're in for a surprise."

"Surprise?" the Marquis queried.

Jenkins nodded.

"The servants won't say anythin' to me in case I should tell your Lordship, I was soon aware of that. There's women here. I sees some of them as I comes down the passage and there's some sort of performance tonight."

Jenkins knew nothing more, but, as the Marquis dressed himself, he thought that he was glad that he had followed his instinct in accepting the Duchess's invitation rather than listen to Charlie.

At least the evening might be original, whilst dinner at Newmarket, although enjoyable, would be very much like all the others he had given in his house.

He tied his cravat in the very latest style and in a manner that was the envy of the dandies.

He did not wear knee breeches, but instead the stovepipe pantaloons that had been introduced by the Prince Regent and which were, the Marquis thought, in the country far more comfortable than silk stockings.

Because he was so tall and looked so impressive, although he was unaware of it, the footmen in the hall, and there was a long line of them, gazed at him admiringly as he came down the stairs.

He would have been surprised if he had heard one of them whisper to the other,

"He be a sportsman, that he be, and too good to be mixed up in this sewer!"

"I agrees with you," the other one replied out of the corner of his mouth.

There were more people in the salon than there had been when the Marquis had first arrived and, if the Duchess had looked fantastic before, then now she was positively dazzling.

She wore a gown of green sequins, the colour of her eyelids. It was not only cut outrageously low in the front but it fitted her almost like a skin and in any drawing room would have been considered unduly provocative if not indecent.

As she moved, a train rustled behind her and the Marquis thought to himself how he would tell Charlie later that she definitely was a serpent and there was no other way to describe her.

She wore an emerald tiara in her red hair, huge emerald earrings swung from her ears and, as she glittered with every movement she made, the Marquis could understand how it was difficult for the men watching her to look at any other woman in the room.

When he saw the other women, he could understand that they had been chosen because they were so different from their hostess.

"I am not going to introduce you to a lot of people who I am sure you know already," the Duchess was speaking again in that low seductive voice he found was very much in keeping with her appearance. "Instead, I am going to present to you a young woman who will look after you this evening, will make sure that you enjoy yourself and be happy to do *anything* you require of her."

The way the Duchess accentuated the word *anything* told the Marquis exactly what she implied and it brought a cynical smile to his lips.

'So that is what is going on,' he told himself and thought that it was what he might have expected.

"This is Aspasia Stanton," the Duchess was saying, "and I do hope you will have a very happy evening together."

She pulled Aspasia forward as she spoke, but the Marquis was not aware that the Duchess's pressure on Aspasia's fingers told her again as sharply and clearly as Mrs. Fielding had said to her in words.

Aspasia was frightened, very frightened, but she knew that she had to hide it and she managed to curtsey while her eyes looked up at the Marquis almost frantically to see what he was like.

She did not know what she had expected.

She had merely been told over and over again that she was to please the gentleman with whom she would spend the evening. She was to amuse and entertain him. She was to do anything he asked of her and in return her uncle could stay on at Little Medlock.

"You are not to talk about yourself," Mrs. Fielding said sharply. "Flatter the gentleman you are with. Tell him how handsome and clever he is and make sure that he finds you desirable."

Aspasia wondered to herself what she meant by that, but she had no chance to ask her any questions.

Mrs. Fielding's method of instructions while she was being dressed was to reiterate over and over again that she must do whatever was expected of her.

When the gown she was to wear was brought from the wardrobe by one of the servants on Mrs. Fielding's instructions, Aspasia had thought that it was the prettiest she had ever seen.

Of white tulle, caught around the hem and on the shoulders with bunches of snowdrops, it made Aspasia think that it was the kind of gown that Persephone might have worn when she came back from the darkness of Hades to herald spring.

When she put it on, however, she thought that it was far too low in the front to be decent, but, when she begged Mrs. Fielding to raise it in some way, the woman merely laughed.

"What are you being so modest about?" she asked. "You've got a pretty figure and there'll be plenty of men to tell you so before you're much older."

Aspasia tried not to look shocked. She knew that it was the sort of thing that she had not only never heard before but was something no respectful servant would say.

But, while Mrs. Fielding looked like a servant, she obviously had a position of authority.

She kept ringing bells and calling for maids who came hurrying to obey her, but the more she talked the more Aspasia realised that she had a common voice and a vulgar way of saying things that her mother would not have approved of.

Then she had been given a bath, which she enjoyed because it was scented with violets, and the same perfume was rubbed into her skin and sprinkled on her hair.

"Do you make this in your still room?" she had asked. "I know that there are plenty of violets in the woods around here."

"We've no time for things like that," Mrs. Fielding replied. "This comes from Jermyn Street in London and a nice price we pays for it too."

"It is very kind of you to let me use it," Aspasia said.

She thought when she was ready that the scent was slightly overpowering and she hoped that it would gradually vanish when she moved about.

When she was dry, one of the maids brought her a pair of silk stockings that made her exclaim in delight.

She had never worn silk stockings before and they fitted closely to her legs and were fastened just above the knee with white satin garters that had little snowdrops attached to them.

"How pretty!" Aspasia exclaimed.

Then Mrs. Fielding took the bath towel away from her and she felt embarrassed at being naked and looked around for her underclothes.

But instead to her surprise the maid brought the white gown with the snowdrops and it was lifted over her head.

"But – I have nothing underneath yet," she protested.

"You don't need anything," Mrs. Fielding said. "It's hot in the dining room and dresses fits better when you're not encumbered with chemises and petticoats."

Aspasia knew that her mother would not approve, but Mrs. Fielding was once again instructing her on her behaviour and before she knew what was happening her gown was buttoned up at the back and only when she looked in the mirror did she realise how very low it was.

She tried to tug it up, but it was too tight at the waist.

"Now leave it alone!" Mrs. Fielding admonished her. "It looks very nice."

"But it is – indecent!"

"Nonsense."

Whatever she said Mrs. Fielding would not listen and Aspasia tried to console herself with the fact that perhaps, as she was unimportant, nobody would look at her anyway, except, of course, the strange man she had to devote herself to for the whole evening.

She wondered what she would do if he was ugly and debauched.

Although she had not told Jerry, she had heard some of the villagers talking to Martha in the kitchen a little time ago and, although she had not meant to listen, she had heard what the woman said,

"Disgustin', I calls it! The Vicar ought to stop it, that's what he ought to do."

"It's none of his business," Martha replied.

"It's everybody's business when gentlemen gets drunk and behaves like animals and when women who are no better than they ought to be are brought down from London. It's a disgrace in a Christian community, that's what it is."

"It's none of our business," Martha had said again in an uncompromising voice.

"It's an abomination and the work of the Devil! And I've always said as those as don't protest against sin when they sees it are sinners themselves!"

"If you are prepared to protest, we are not!" Martha said, "And the less we talk about it, Mrs. Briggs, the better!"

Aspasia had forgotten the conversation, but now she remembered what Mrs. Briggs had said and, although she had very seldom seen anybody the worse for drink, she knew that it was frightening and something that she would have no idea of how to cope with.

Now, as she looked up at the Marquis, she thought that he was the most handsome man she had ever seen in her whole life, even better-looking than Jerry, and she knew, whatever else he might be, that he was not a drunkard.

But he was overpowering and she thought despairingly that she would never be able to interest him and certainly not amuse him in the way that Mrs. Fielding expected of her.

She saw too that there was a cynical twist to his lips and thought for a while that he was amused by what was happening and perhaps by her appearance, but his attitude was not particularly complimentary.

Aspasia was offered a glass of champagne and, although she wished to refuse it, she thought perhaps it would give her courage and took it with a hand that trembled.

The Duchess moved away and the Marquis said in a voice that she thought was deep and somehow attractive,

"Well, Miss Stanton, as this is my first visit here you must tell me what to expect."

"I don't – know myself," Aspasia answered. "I only came – here this evening."

"So you have come here from London," the Marquis remarked and she thought it best not to contradict him.

Mrs. Fielding had been most insistent that she was not to talk about herself.

She took a sip of the champagne and thought the taste disappointing.

It was a wine that she had never drunk before and had always imagined, because people talked about it as being so delicious, that it would be sparkling, which it was but also sweet and succulent.

She did not like to put down the glass, but stood holding it, her eyes on the Marquis.

"You must tell me about yourself," he said. "What do you do when you are in London?"

"I would much – rather talk about – you," Aspasia said. "Will you tell me your – name?"

"Of course," the Marquis replied, "we were very inadequately introduced. I am the Marquis of Thame."

Aspasia's eyes lit up.

"Then you own some very splendid horses."

"You know about them?"

"But of course."

She did not add that living near Newmarket there was nobody even in Little Medlock who was not aware of the horses that were trained there.

Jerry, when he was at home, took the racing papers and followed the methods of the trainers who they knew by name with an enthusiasm that Aspasia found infectious.

They had always shared everything together and she shared this interest as she shared his others.

Although Martha disapproved, they went to the races when they took place and in the last two years she had seen the Marquis's horses carry off the best prizes.

"Are you really interested in racing?" the Marquis was asking now, "or is it the bets that are put on for you by your admirers that make you find 'The Sport of Kings' so enticing?"

But Aspasia was not listening.

"I thought the race won by your horse, Conqueror, was one of the most exciting I have ever watched."

"You were there?" the Marquis asked in surprise.

"For one moment he was boxed in, but your jockey was clever enough to come up on the outside and when he won by half a length it was the most thrilling thing that ever happened in any race."

There was an enthusiasm in her voice that the Marquis knew was sincere and they talked about his horses until it was time to go into dinner.

When they were seated in the large dining room where the Duchess's ancestors looked down at them from their portraits on the walls, the Marquis glanced around the table to take stock of the other guests.

There were twenty in all and he recognised many of the men as characters he had gone out of his way to avoid in London and whom he would not have invited to his own house under any circumstances.

As Charlie had anticipated, Dagenham was there looking more dissolute than ever, but he was easily rivalled by several other middle-aged men whose reputations were as disreputable as his if not worse.

Besides Dagenham there were several rather stupid young wasters who were throwing away their fortunes either at cards or on women whom the more experienced men avoided.

To each of the gentlemen at the table there was a girl attached in the same way, the Marquis realised, as Aspasia was attached to him.

He noticed that the Duchess had obviously chosen her guest's partners with some forethought.

Dagenham had a woman with him who looked young, but from the way she was behaving the Marquis reckoned that she was an expert in the 'exotic' pleasures that revolted him.

The other male guests were partnered by sophisticated creatures whom, if nothing else, would have an expertise in extracting from their pockets every possible pound they owned.

The Marquis knew exactly why he had been given someone as young and fresh-looking as Aspasia.

He had not been one of the youngest Commanders of troops in the Duke of Wellington's Army without being able to assess a man's character shrewdly and unerringly and, while he did not pretend to be as expert with women, he found when he used his instinct as well as his knowledge of humanity that he was seldom wrong in his assessment.

Looking at the Duchess sitting at the top of the table glittering with emeralds and having the appearance of a hooded cobra he was prepared to salute her for her perception.

She had taken the trouble to reason out for herself with what he knew was a sharp and intelligent mind exactly what a man needed and desired and was determined to provide it.

The Marquis was certain she thought that this was the only way she could preserve her power.

It had been easy when she was young and beautiful to fill the house with men who now no longer came for her personally, but for what she could provide.

At the same time the two foreigners on either side of her were fawning over her and paying her compliments. She was enticing them with her eyes, her lips, the sensuous movements of her body and, the Marquis was certain, inflammatory words.

He could only find the whole play unrolling in front of him was both intriguing and entertaining.

Now he could understand why the Duchess was spoken about with bated breath and why he had been warned against her.

'Fortunately,' the Marquis told himself, 'I am too clever to be caught in such a trap.'

He was certain that it was one.

He had complained and instead of answering his complaints she had decided to force him into her clutches and to make herself indispensable to his needs, as she had obviously done with the other men sitting round the table.

There was a very cynical look in the Marquis's eyes as he turned his attention once again to Aspasia.

She certainly looked the part of being a very young, pure and innocent virgin which would attract a man because she was the exact opposite of the sophisticated women who he occupied his time in London with.

What was more he had already realised that she was a consummate actress.

Her nervous little manner when they first met, the question in her eyes as if she was afraid of him as a man, were all so well acted that he felt sure that if she was on the stage she would soon make her name.

But he assumed that she had chosen an older and more obvious profession and he thought that by the end of the evening he would be able to catch her out and that he would find her not as innocent as she pretended and undoubtedly not as pure as she looked.

For one thing her gown was too low and for another the flames in her hair made the Marquis feel that it would be impossible for her to escape the fires of Venus although for the moment she was keeping them well under control.

When he looked at her, he realised that she was staring round the table in surprise and, as she looked at the Duchess at the end of it, she looked away quickly and said,

"Please let us go on talking about your horses."

"I have a feeling that we have rather exhausted that subject," the Marquis replied. "What else interests you?"

"The pictures in this house," Aspasia replied. "When I arrived, there was a Rubens in the room that I was shown into and the colours are even more beautiful than I ever anticipated they would be."

"Who told you that it was a Rubens?" he asked.

"I knew," she answered, "but it was also marked underneath."

"Now confess," the Marquis said, "you looked at the artist's name first."

"I think I should have been very stupid not to be able to recognise a Rubens," Aspasia protested. "His colours are painted in a very different way from other artists. But Poussin is more difficult and I did have to guess when I saw one in the same room. Then when I was near enough to read the artist's name on the frame I saw that I had guessed correctly."

"You surprise me," the Marquis said.

He spoke a little dryly as if he did not believe her and Aspasia remembered that she was not talking about him.

"Do you possess many pictures?" she asked him.

"A great number," he replied, "and some of them are particularly fine."

"I should – love to see them."

This, the Marquis thought, was the sort of hint he would expect to come later in the evening, but he merely smiled as he replied,

"It might be possible. We shall have to see."

Aspasia realised that it was completely impossible, but perhaps it would be a good thing to pretend.

"I have seen pictures in the museum at Cambridge," she went on, "and, while there are not many of them, some of them are very beautiful."

"Why were you in Cambridge?" the Marquis asked. "You told me that you had never been here before."

"This is my first visit to Grimstone House."

He thought that the way she spoke was very convincing. He was certain that she was putting on an act, but was finding it difficult to catch her out.

The food was delicious. In fact the Marquis when comparing the efforts of his own chefs was not certain that the Duchess had not beaten him in the culinary stakes. The wine too was superlative.

Charlie had been completely wrong. The claret was outstanding and the white wine superior to anything that the Marquis had savoured at Carlton House.

Of one thing, however, he was aware of very early in the evening and that was that nobody's glass at the table was ever empty for one moment. The servants continually refilled them every time a diner took so much as a sip.

It was quite obvious that the Duchess's guests made the most of the excellent fare and drink that they were provided with.

Voices grew louder, faces grew redder and, although the Marquis held up his hand to prevent his glass from being refilled every time he drank from it, the servants obviously had their orders and ignored him.

He noticed, however, that Aspasia was drinking nothing.

He had been aware as he had given her his arm to take her into dinner that when she put down her glass of champagne it was still full.

Now he noticed that she had three glasses in front of her, all of them untouched.

"You are not thirsty?" he asked.

"I am," she replied, "but I feel if I ask just for water it will look rude."

"Perhaps you would like some lemonade?"

"I would love some, but would they not think it strange?"

The Marquis thought that she was again playing her part of being ingenuous, but he turned his head to the servant standing behind his chair.

"Bring this young lady a glass of lemonade."

"I don't think there is any, my Lord."

"Then find some!" the Marquis said sharply.

As if he obeyed the voice of authority, the man hurried away, but Aspasia looked at the Marquis with a worried expression in her eyes.

"Perhaps the Duchess will be – angry."

The Marquis smiled.

"Let her be!"

"I-I cannot do – that."

"Why not?"

Aspasia looked at the end of the table.

"Please – please be very careful – if I do anything to make her – annoyed it – will be terrible."

"I cannot think that a glass of lemonade could have such a devastating effect."

"One – never knows," Aspasia replied in a little above a whisper.

Then, as if she felt that she had said too much, she said quickly,

"But – I want you to enjoy yourself – how can I make sure that you do so?"

"Perhaps we can talk about that later," the Marquis replied with a faint smile.

CHAPTER THREE

The dinner came to an end and, as the table was cleared, the Marquis looked around once again at the other guests and saw that the majority of the gentlemen had had too much to drink and so had some of the women.

This resulted in their behaving in a very familiar manner with one another and he thought that what would happen for the rest of the evening was very predictable and bore out Charlie's contention that it would not amuse him.

The two foreign men on either side of the Duchess were obviously flattering her and whispering intimacies into her ears, vying with each other doubtless to excite her.

She was actually, the Marquis thought, the only woman in the room who was being enticed rather than attempting to entice, with the exception, of course, of Aspasia, who had been allotted to him.

He looked down at her and then realised that she was staring at the other guests with an expression which seemed to be one of shocked surprise.

Then he told himself that it was all part of her very clever act and he would be half-witted if he was deceived by it.

He looked again at the Duchess and realised that she was gazing at him. He thought perhaps that she was suspecting him of being critical and it was something that would not augur well for their discussions tomorrow.

He picked up his glass of champagne, which he had hardly touched. In fact he had deliberately drunk very little the whole evening.

He had only taken a sip of it when the respectful voice of a servant came from behind his chair,

"Her Grace's compliments, my Lord, and she hopes you'll join her in a toast."

As the man spoke, he set down on the table a glass containing what appeared to be brandy, but almost instinctively the Marquis was on his guard.

His inner instinct had never failed him when he sensed that there was danger. It had saved his life on several occasions during the War and he knew now in a manner that he could not explain to himself that it would be a great mistake to drink the wine that the Duchess had sent for him.

He had already suspected that some of the guests at the table were under the influence of drugs and he knew that there were places in London where they were used to stimulate elderly men and to make women more compliant.

The Marquis thought quickly and then he raised his glass in the direction of the Duchess who, as he expected, was still looking at him.

She too had a glass in her hand and, as if she pointed the way, she raised it to her lips.

The Marquis made as if he would do the same. Then he smiled at his hostess and looked down at Aspasia and raised his glass to her.

"You have very beautiful blue eyes," he said, "and your hair has captured the sunshine."

He spoke in a clear voice and then beneath his breath so that only Aspasia could hear he said,

"Drop your handkerchief on the floor!"

She looked at him in astonishment and he said again loudly,

"I am toasting you, Aspasia." Then quietly, "do as I say."

Obediently Aspasia took the lace-edged handkerchief that was in her lap and which she had carried in her hand when she came downstairs and dropped it on the floor between herself and the Marquis.

Because she felt that was what he expected her to do she looked down at it and even as he lifted his glass to his lips he followed the direction of her eyes and bent forward to see what had happened.

"You have dropped your handkerchief!" he exclaimed. "Let me pick it up for you."

He bent below the table and so swiftly that Aspasia thought she must have been mistaken in what she saw, he tipped the wine from his glass onto the thick carpet.

Then he sat up, Aspasia's handkerchief in his left hand, which he gave to her.

As he did so, he carried the now empty glass to his lips and appeared to tip its whole contents down his throat, throwing back his head to do so.

Then he held up the empty glass in the direction of the Duchess as if he had completed his toast to her.

She smiled her acknowledgement.

Then, as the Marquis leaned back against his chair, wondering what effect if he had drunk the wine it would have had on him, the music of a hidden orchestra started to play.

Servants lifted the candelabra from the table and snuffed out the candles and for a moment the whole dining room was in darkness.

There were cries of surprise from the guests before a second later at the far end of the room two red velvet curtains were thrown back.

Now there was light again, but it came from footlights concealed by flowers that illuminated a small stage raised almost to the level of the guests' eyes, profusely decorated with flowers it had a human tableau in the centre of it.

One glance told the Marquis exactly what to expect and he recognised a posture from the *Kama Sutra* performed by two girls and a man all of them completely naked.

There were cheers from the guests watching and those who were capable of it clapped their hands in appreciation.

The Marquis thought, as after a few seconds of immobility the performers began to move, that once again Charlie had been right and what they were going to watch would doubtless make him feel, if not sick, then certainly disgusted.

He had always hated obscenity of any sort, just as he disliked dirty jokes, which he did not consider witty and he thought that as the whole evening had been leading up to this the finale would doubtless be an orgy that he had no intention of taking part in.

He was just wondering what would happen if he rose from the table and walked out of the dining room when a small frightened voice beside him said,

"They are – naked! How can – women appear – naked in such an – indecent manner?"

As she spoke, the Marquis realised that he had forgotten Aspasia.

Now he saw that she was not looking at the stage, but down at her hands, which were clenched together in her lap and he thought, although he could not be sure, that her face was very pale.

"I gather that this is something you did not expect," he remarked.

"Expect?" she replied. "How could – anybody expect a – lady to permit people to appear – naked in her dining room?"

She sounded so horrified that the Marquis felt that she really must be sincere and yet he could not be sure that it was not part of the Duchess's plan to make him feel that she was a very young and innocent girl who was different from the rest of the party.

He put his elbow on the table and turned round so that he blocked Aspasia's view of the stage before he said,

"Look at me, Aspasia."

She hesitated as if she was afraid of what she would see.

Then, as if she must obey him, she slowly raised her eyes and looked up.

The Marquis saw that she was indeed very pale and her eyes had a stricken look in them that he could not misunderstand it and was certainly an expression that she could not fake.

"Please," Aspasia said pleadingly, "please – please let me go – away! I cannot – stay here! It is – wrong and wicked and I know now that the stories I have heard were – true although I would not – believe them."

She spoke in a low frightened voice that was little above a whisper.

"What will happen if you show that you are shocked by leaving the room?" the Marquis asked her.

"I cannot – tell you," Aspasia replied. "I promised on my – sacred word of honour that I would – stay with you and – amuse you and if it does – amuse you – then there is nothing I – can do."

She paused and then she closed her eyes again and said,

"I cannot – I will not – look!"

The Marquis turned his head in the direction of the stage.

As he expected, the three actors had now been joined by two more and the way that they were behaving was certainly touching the depths of obscenity that exceeded anything that he had seen anywhere else in the world.

He looked around the room and then realised that excited by the spectacle on top of the amount of drink they had consumed a couple who had been clasped passionately in each other's arms were now moving towards the door as if they would find a more private place to continue their involvement with each other.

He looked back again at Aspasia.

Her eyes were still closed, but her lips were moving and he had the feeling, although he mocked at himself for thinking so, that she was praying.

"Listen to me, Aspasia," he said. "I can take you out of this room without anybody thinking it strange that you are running away from the entertainment that has been provided for us."

She gave a little cry that was almost one of delight and she half-opened her eyes as if afraid of what she would see and then opened them a little wider when she realised that her vision of the stage was still obscured by the Marquis.

"The only way we can do this," he went on, "is to make the Duchess think that we want to be alone together."

He saw that she was listening and he continued,

"You have doubtless noticed that all the other guests are behaving very intimately with one another, so I am going to put my arms around you, hold you close to me and then I will draw you to your feet so that we can move towards the door."

His voice sharpened as he went on,

"Our hostess must think that I have drunk too much, so I must appear to be a little unsteady. Do you understand? It is the only way that we can leave without causing a great deal of comment."

"I – understand," Aspasia said. "Please – please let's go away – at once!"

"Very well," the Marquis murmured.

He reached out as he spoke and drew her against him so it appeared as if he was kissing first her hair and then her forehead.

As he did so, he felt her tremble. She hid her face against his shoulder and because she was very frightened one hand clutched at the lapel of his evening coat.

For some seconds he just held her, hoping that their embrace was being noticed by the Duchess.

Then he pushed back his chair and said in a voice that could be overheard by the servants,

"Let'sh get out of here and go sh-omewhere more comfortable."

He deliberately slurred his words and then walking with the careful deliberate gait of a man who is not quite sure that his feet will obey him, the Marquis moved slowly, holding Aspasia tightly against him, towards the door.

To reach it they had to pass either behind the Duchess's chair at one end of the room or in front of the stage.

As they did so, the Marquis could not help noticing what was taking place behind the footlights and he thought that it would be hard to make even Charlie believe that such filth could be portrayed in England and in a house that belonged to a family who had played their part in the history of the country.

They reached the door and stepped out into the corridor and the Marquis knew as he did so that Aspasia would have moved away from him.

But he said quietly,

"There are still the servants watching us, and I suggest you stay close to me until we can be sure that nobody will report to our hostess anything we do."

"Y-yes – of course," Aspasia replied.

She clung to him and he kept his arm around her until they came to the end of the passage, and reached the hall.

They climbed the wide staircase slowly and, when they reached the top, Aspasia felt that at last she had escaped from the horrors of the dining room.

She was just about to say so when, as the Marquis turned down the passage, she saw in the shadows of a doorway watching them was Mrs. Fielding.

She felt her heart give a sudden leap of fear and having raised her head from the Marquis's shoulder she hesitatingly put it back as they walked for what seemed to her to be a long way down the corridor before they stopped at a door.

The Marquis opened it and only when they had entered and he closed it behind them did Aspasia feel him straighten himself to his full height.

"Thank God we are away from that muck hole!" he said in his ordinary voice. "How in God's name did you get mixed up in anything like this?"

Aspasia did not answer and he realised that she was staring not at him but at the big four-poster in the centre of the room.

It was a very magnificent bed draped with red silk curtains and above the pillows there was emblazoned the Grimstone Coat of Arms.

The lights in the room came only from two candelabra one on either side of the bed, but there was enough light to see the painted ceiling, the windows with their carved and gilt pelmets and that the furniture was spectacular.

"I have been comfortably housed, as you can see," the Marquis commented.

Aspasia turned to look at him.

"B-but it is – your bedroom." she said in a low tone.

"That is obvious."

"But – where am I to sleep?"

He looked to see if what she was saying was true and then replied,

"I should have thought that was obvious too."

For a moment Aspasia was very still. Then she gave a little cry that was one of sheer horror and ran towards the door.

She turned the handle and then, as she would have pulled it towards her, she remembered Mrs. Fielding.

She would still be there watching to make certain that she kept her sacred word of honour and did everything the Marquis asked of her.

She left the door, sped across to the nearest window and, pulling aside the curtains, looked out.

The casement was open and the moonlight illuminating the garden outside made it easy for Aspasia to see at a glance that, although the bedroom was on the first floor, it was in a part of the house where the rooms were high up and so there was a long drop to the ground.

She stood, however, looking down wondering frantically what she should do until she heard the Marquis say behind her,

"Perhaps you had better tell me what all this commotion is about."

He spoke in a dry commanding voice and because it was so impersonal it was somehow reassuring and took away a little of Aspasia's fear.

She turned back to the room and stood still, her hands clasped together.

"P-please – try to understand," she said, "when I promised I would – do what you wanted – I had no idea, it never – occurred to me – that the Duchess or Mrs. Fielding could – mean anything like – this."

She was trembling as she said the last word and she looked the same way, the Marquis thought, as she had looked at the naked performers on the stage.

He did not speak and she went on,

"I did not know – what you would – ask me to do – but it is wrong – and wicked for two people to – sleep in the same bed – if they are not – married!"

The Marquis, who had been standing ever since they had come into the bedroom, walked to the bed and sat down on the side of the mattress. He looked elegant and very masculine silhouetted against the Grimstone Coat of Arms.

But, because he was on the bed, Aspasia trembled and she felt as if her lips were dry and that anything more she might have been about to say was already strangled in her throat.

She knew that the Marquis was watching her and for the moment she thought that he was like an animal who might spring on her and she would not be able to escape him.

Then he said again in his dry quiet voice,

"I think, Aspasia, you have a good deal of explaining to do and I suggest that you sit down in a chair and try to stop being so frightened."

"But – I am frightened and – perhaps I shall not be able to make you – understand."

"I promise that I will try to do so and the easiest way is for you to tell me the truth."

"They – told me I was not – to do that."

"By 'they' I presume you mean the Duchess and the woman we saw watching us as we came down the corridor."

"Yes – that is – Mrs. Fielding."

"Well, she is not likely to know what is happening inside this room," the Marquis pointed out, "so we can talk here without being concerned that we might be overhead."

"Are you – certain of – that?"

"Yes!"

The Marquis felt that the positive way he spoke convinced Aspasia and, as if she had remembered that he had told her to sit down, she moved towards an armchair beside the fireplace.

He was aware that it was as far away from him as it was possible for her to be.

Only after she had seated herself did he rise from the bed to take the chair opposite her.

He thought she glanced at him as he did so as if she was terrified and he then said,

"It will be easier if we are nearer to each other, so that there is no need for us to raise our voices."

"Yes – of course."

There was silence and after a moment the Marquis spoke,

"You had better start at the very beginning. Who are you and what is your real name?"

"I am Aspasia Stanton!"

"You were christened 'Aspasia'?" he questioned. "It seems rather a strange name for an English girl."

"It was chosen by my uncle who is a Greek scholar and it means 'welcome'."

The Marquis was surprised that she should have known that and he continued,

"And you live in London?"

"No, I live here with my uncle, who is the Vicar of Little Medlock."

"The Vicar? And he allowed you to come to a house like this?"

"He – does not know I am – here."

"Then what was the reason, was it curiosity? Or was it because you needed the money?"

He saw the surprise in Aspasia's eyes before she replied,

"It was – nothing like that. It was something that – happened at breakfast – this morning."

"What was that?"

"There was a letter for Uncle Theophilus and as he was busy he told me to open it."

Slowly, prompted by questions from the Marquis, Aspasia related what the letter contained and how, after her uncle had gone with Martha to bury her sister, she had decided she would come to Grimstone to beg the Duchess to change her mind and let him stay on in the Parish,

The only thing she was careful not to mention was that she had a brother and that it was Jerry who had ridden with her as far as he dared before he had returned home.

She told the Marquis how she had pleaded with the Duchess who had told her that she intended to have only young people about her because old age was infectious.

Then because someone was ill, Aspasia was not certain who, the Duchess had said that if she took her place and stayed the night and did exactly what she was told without fuss or complaint her uncle could keep his Living.

"Of course I – agreed," she said. "It seemed so – wonderful that I was able to – save Uncle Theophilus and he would not have to find somewhere else to – live."

"But you did not expect a dinner party like the one you have just attended?" the Marquis asked.

"How could I think – people would – behave in such a disgusting – manner?" Aspasia asked in a low shocked voice. "The gentlemen had – drunk too much, and so had – some of the women."

"Did you meet any of them before dinner?"

"No – I did not even know that they were here until I came downstairs to the salon. The only person I saw was Mrs. Fielding and the maids who helped me to dress."

"So your gown belongs to the Duchess."

"Yes. It was she who told Mrs. Fielding what I was to wear and I remember her saying, 'That one always works with the more sophisticated ones'."

It all began to fit into place, the Marquis thought, and he was beginning to see the whole pattern of the Duchess's plans to ensnare him as she had ensnared the other fools downstairs with drinks, drugs, women and obscenity.

It was the sort of thing that quite a number of men who frequented the *Beau Monde* would find an irresistible attraction.

But the Duchess could not have known, because she had never met him, that there was nothing in her house that was likely to be of the least interest to him, except perhaps Aspasia.

He had known when he first saw her that she was surprisingly lovely. He had never seen her colour of hair on any other woman and her small pointed face and huge dark blue eyes would, he thought, have been irresistibly alluring even among the beauties who frequented Carlton House.

But the circumstances that they met in had led him to assume that she was a clever actress, well rehearsed in the part she had to play, and that her air of innocence was over-accentuated by the way she was dressed.

Now listening to her the Marquis could hardly believe that he was not still being deceived so subtly that he would be a fool not to be suspicious.

And yet every word that Aspasia had said seemed to ring true. As he watched her he knew her fear could not be anything but real and the eyes she turned beseechingly up to him were innocent and bewildered.

As she came to the end of her tale, she added,

"There have been strange – rumours in Little Medlock, but nobody there has any – idea of the real – wickedness that is taking place – here."

"What other things do they talk about?" the Marquis said.

"The things that happen on the other parts of the estate," Aspasia replied, "but I would rather not tell you about them."

The Marquis did not press her, he only asked,

"What do you want to do now?"

"I want to go home – I want to leave here and never come back – never! *Never!*"

"If you do leave so soon," the Marquis said, "the Duchess will think that you have not kept your part of the contract."

There was silence and then Aspasia once again in a terrified little voice said,

"Y-you mean – if I do not stay here with you – she will make Uncle Theophilus leave in a month's time?"

"I think that is likely," the Marquis responded.

"But – I cannot – you don't – understand – I cannot stay."

The Marquis realised that it was only by a tremendous effort of will that she did not jump to her feet and once again she was frightened to the point where she was thinking despairingly that to escape she might have to throw herself out of the window.

He did not know how he knew that this was in her thoughts.

But he thought that her eyes were transparent with the clearness of a stream or perhaps, where she was concerned, he was even more perceptive as to her feelings than he usually was when he was interrogating anybody.

"Let me promise you one thing," he said, "I will not do anything that you would not wish me to do."

As he spoke, he knew that Aspasia's fears subsided as if they were the waves of a rough sea and after a moment she asked,

"Do you – really mean – that? You will – not – touch me?"

"Not unless you ask me to do so," the Marquis replied with a smile, "and, as that is very unlikely, it seems pointless to talk about it."

"Thank you – thank you very – much," Aspasia said in a breathless little voice.

"Now what we have to decide together," the Marquis said in a different tone, "is how you can make the Duchess certain that you have kept your promise to her and therefore she must keep hers."

"Please – tell me how – I can do it?"

"I have been thinking," he answered, "that having seen Mrs. Fielding keeping guard outside, you will have to stay here at least for a part of the night. There is plenty of room for us both to be quite comfortable."

"Yes – yes – of course," Aspasia agreed.

"And I imagine about dawn," the Marquis went on, "you can go back to your own room."

Aspasia considered this for a moment.

And then she said,

"I don't know where my own room is. I changed my gown down a long passage in the opposite direction from this and I thought that when you – arranged to go to bed and had no – further use for me – you would send a – servant to show me – the way."

Because Aspasia sounded a little incoherent the Marquis added,

"In that case forget it and I imagine that you would rather go home than have any further communication with Mrs. Fielding or the Duchess."

"I-I could not – bear to see – either of them again," Aspasia said passionately. "I know now they are both – wicked – horrible women to have arranged that those people should appear – naked in the – dining room."

The Marquis realised that it was simply their nakedness that had upset Aspasia. Because she was so innocent, she had no idea that the fact that they were wearing nothing was a very minor part of the degradation of their act.

"Forget it!" he exclaimed. "It is something that you should not have seen and are never likely to see again. Just put it out of your mind."

"I – will – try," Aspasia said humbly, "and I hope too I can forget – the Duchess and – Mrs. Fielding."

"You must try," the Marquis went on firmly. "Now we must both make an effort to sleep as comfortably as we can and I think, Aspasia, that we would be very stupid if we did not avail ourselves of that very large and comfortable bed."

He saw her stiffen and went on,

"I will lie on one side of it and you on the other and we will put a pillow between us. As soon as it is dawn and it is not likely that there will be anybody about, I will take you home. I presume the Duchess intended to send you back in her carriage, but it would be best for you not to wake her up."

"I could not – bear it," Aspasia replied, "she might – ask me to do – something else – and all I want to do is to – get away."

"I can understand that," the Marquis agreed, "and I suggest you sit down at that desk and write her a note saying that as you have fulfilled your promise and done everything that I required and you are therefore going home."

He paused before he added sarcastically,

"You will then thank her for having promised that your uncle may keep his Living."

Aspasia drew in her breath.

"That is clever of you – very clever," she said. "Shall I write it now?"

"Yes," the Marquis replied, "and, as we have a long and not very comfortable night before us, I hope you will forgive me if I take off my evening coat."

"Y-yes – of course."

He knew, however, as she moved towards the French secrétaire that she was not thinking of him but of the letter she had to write.

She did not take long in doing so and, when she had finished, she turned round to find that the Marquis had extinguished the lights on one side of the bed and was now lying on it, propped against the pillows.

He was still wearing his white shirt and long tight-fitting black pantaloons, but he had loosened his cravat and he appeared to be very much at his ease and not nearly so frightening as he had seemed before.

Aspasia stood briefly gazing at him.

Then she saw that one of the lace pillows from the bed lay beside him and beyond it there was plenty of room for her without there being the slightest chance of her brushing against him.

She laid the letter down on the secrétaire and walked a little nearer to the bed as she said,

"I have just been thinking – it is very kind of you to say that you will take me home tomorrow – but I have nothing to – wear except for this – gown I have on now."

"I expect I can find you something to put over it," the Marquis replied, "but, as it is late and you are tired, I suggest that you now try to sleep. I promise I will wake you as soon as it is possible for us to leave."

"You are – quite sure you will not oversleep?"

"I have been a soldier, Aspasia, and I have taught myself to wake up when I want to."

She gave him a little smile, then because he realised that she was shy and the colour was rising in her cheeks, he turned on his side with his back to the centre of the bed and closed his eyes.

"Hurry up, Aspasia," he said in the same tone that Jerry might have used to her. "I am sleepy and I want to put out the light."

Aspasia did as she was told and walking round the bed climbed in on the other side.

As she put her head against the pillows, she realised that they were very soft and after all she had been through today she was definitely very tired.

She slipped off the satin slippers that were a size too big for her, but were the smallest that Mrs. Fielding could find and, giving them a little push, heard them fall to the floor.

Then she closed her eyes.

She heard the Marquis blow out the candles one by one and then they lay in the dark.

"Goodnight, Aspasia," he said. "Sleep well."

"I will – try," she answered, "and I am going to thank God in my prayers because you have been so – very – very kind to me."

There was silence before she added,

"Supposing you had been – like one of those – other men who drank too much – and who applauded – the naked people on the stage?"

The fear was now back in her voice.

"But I am not," the Marquis replied, "so go to sleep, Aspasia."

"Thank you – for being – you," she whispered and started to say her prayers.

CHAPTER FOUR

Aspasia awoke suddenly and wondered for a moment where she was. Then she realised that somebody had pulled back the curtains and she could see the pale yellow dawn moving up the sky while there were still twinkling some stars overhead.

She stared at them for a moment and then heard a sound and realised what had awoken her.

The Marquis was in the bathroom.

At the thought of him she sat up quickly feeling that it was incredible that she had in fact slept dreamlessly while lying on a bed beside a strange man.

Then she saw the pillow between them and that on his side the sheet was creased where he had lain all night.

It struck her once again how fortunate she had been in being with a man who had no interest in her.

The way the other gentlemen were behaving at the end of dinner made her aware that if she had been with one of them it would have been preferable to throw herself from the window than to stay.

She climbed out of bed feeling that what she needed was air. Her lips felt dry and she was thirsty.

Despite the Marquis's order she had never been brought the lemonade that she had asked for last night.

Then, as she reached the centre of the room, she glanced without thinking towards the mantelpiece and stood still.

Over it was a large portrait of a man.

Skilfully painted, obviously by a great artist, he was leaning casually against an ornate urn. At the same time there was something so alive and vital about him that she felt almost as if he might step from the picture and she could speak to him.

She was so spellbound that she did not hear the Marquis come into the room and, when he spoke just behind her, she started.

"I see you are admiring the third Duke," he said. "I have heard that he was a splendid fwllow and I should think if he returned he would be very ashamed of the way that his daughter is behaving."

Aspasia did not reply and the Marquis looked up at the picture to add,

"I wish I had known him, for, if he had been here I am sure that there would have been none of the difficulties we are encountering at the moment."

Still Aspasia did not say anything and the Marquis went on,

"I think we should get away from here as soon as possible if you wish to avoid meeting the Duchess or that woman who was watching us last night."

Aspasia gave a little exclamation of horror and the Marquis ordered her,

"Go and wash the sleep out of your eyes and I will find you something to put over your gown."

She hurried to obey him going quickly into the bathroom, where she not only washed from a ewer of cold water but drank a glass of it.

She saw that the Marquis had bathed by pouring cans of cold water into a silver bath and she thought when she went home that she would do the same and try to wash away the horrors of last night.

She knew that he was right and she must get away as rapidly as possible.

She went back into the bedroom to find that he was just finishing tying his cravat in front of the looking glass.

He was wearing riding breeches with highly polished Hessians and, without turning his head, he told her,

"I have put a cape on the bed that should cover you."

Aspasia saw that what he had provided for her was his black evening cape, which was lined with satin. It had a velvet collar and when she clasped it at her neck it hid her gown except for a few inches at the hem.

"Thank – you," she said. "This will do splendidly. But how are – we to travel?"

"I have been thinking about that," the Marquis replied.

He went to the wardrobe as he spoke and drew out a riding jacket of grey whipcord.

As he put it on, he continued,

"Although they are used to getting up early, my grooms will not be awake at this hour. So, unless there is somebody on duty at the stables, I will saddle my own horse and take you to your home in front of me."

"I am – very sorry to be such a – nuisance," Aspasia said humbly, thinking how uncomfortable it would be for him.

The Marquis smiled before he said,

"Actually, and you may find it hard to believe this, I am enjoying pitting my wits against the Duchess and hoping that I shall be the victor!"

"I am praying very hard that you will be," Aspasia said.

"I am sure that your prayers are always effective," he replied. "Now come along and pray that we will not be seen."

He opened the door of the bedroom cautiously as he spoke and looked down the passage.

As he had expected, the candles in the sconces had gutted low, but there was enough light to see that there was nobody about.

He reached out to take Aspasia by the hand and having closed the door quietly set off down the corridor walking very softly for such a large man.

He avoided the main staircase where peeping through the banisters Aspasia could see that the nightfootman was asleep by the front door in a large padded chair with a high hood.

They walked on and, as the Marquis obviously expected, they came to another secondary staircase, which took them down to the ground floor.

Aspasia thought that if they went much further they would come to the dining room and beyond that must be the kitchen where the servants would soon be starting to cook and clean.

The Marquis discovered a side door that, when he had unbolted it, led them out among some shrubs.

Running through them was a narrow path from which they emerged into a part of the garden that was not far from the stables.

This was where they wanted to be and Aspasia wished to tell the Marquis how clever he had been, but she thought it best not to speak.

She was not to know that the Marquis was extremely pleased with himself for having worked out a plan of the house in his mind and he was delighted at having arrived at exactly the place he intended.

The stable was very quiet and, as the Marquis had anticipated, there was a young groom on duty. He was asleep on a pile of hay in an empty stall.

He woke apologetically when spoken to and obviously expected to be reprimanded only to be delighted, when having saddled the Marquis's stallion, he found himself generously rewarded.

Leading the stallion outside the Marquis lifted Aspasia onto the saddle and swung himself up behind her.

She tried to make herself as small as possible, but he put his left arm around her and pulled her back against him and they set off at quite a good pace, the Marquis managing to keep the stallion under control with one hand.

Only when they were well away from the house did he say and it was the first time he had spoken to Aspasia since they had left the bedroom,

"You will have to direct me."

"I think it would be wisest," she answered, "if you return home the way I came here – which will prevent us from being seen."

"That would certainly be wise," the Marquis agreed, "and when I return I shall say that I took you home because you wished to leave early."

"Must you say – that?"

"I never lie unless it is absolutely necessary."

Aspasia remembered that this was something that her mother had always said,

"I hate and detest lies and untruths of all sorts," she remarked once in her soft voice, "but if we must lie to save somebody's life or just their reputation, then we call them 'white lies' and they are not so reprehensible." Mrs. Stanton paused, before she added, "But even so, they should be convincing and as near to the truth as possible."

Aspasia had been aware what her mother was referring to and she had known that in that particular case the 'white lies' they had to tell were absolutely necessary and therefore forgivable.

They rode on for quite a long way before the Marquis said,

"I have been thinking over what you have told me, Aspasia, and I want you to listen carefully to what I have to say to you."

"Yes, of – course."

She had been thinking how safe she felt with his arms around her and how strong he was, so that for the moment she was no longer afraid.

But she knew that, once she reached home and he was gone, her fears would come back, especially the fear that the Duchess would not keep her word even after she had done what was asked of her and that her uncle would still have to retire and they would have to leave the Vicarage.

Almost as if he followed her thoughts, the Marquis went on,

"I had intended to leave for London this afternoon, but now I shall stay until tomorrow. Therefore if by chance you hear anything that is upsetting you can get in touch with me. You know where my house is in Newmarket?"

"Yes, I know it," Aspasia agreed.

Jerry had pointed it out to her after they had watched Conqueror win two years ago and it was not far from the Marquis's racing stables.

"If I do *not* hear from you by tomorrow morning," the Marquis continued, "then I shall go back to London. Again, if you wish to contact me, anybody will tell you which is my house in Berkeley Square."

"You are very – kind to trouble so much about – me," Aspasia said in a low voice.

"What is more," the Marquis continued, "although it is unlikely after you have fulfilled your promise, if the Duchess does dismiss your uncle, I am sure that I can find him a Living among the many I have in my gift on my estates."

Aspasia gave a little cry and turned her head to look up at him.

"How can you be – so wonderful?" she asked. "Now I am no longer afraid for the future and I feel certain that God has answered my prayers."

"But there is one thing I want you to promise me."

"What is – that?"

"That whatever the Duchess says, whatever orders she may give you, you will not ever go to Grimstone House again."

"No, of course – not," Aspasia replied, and the Marquis felt the shudder that went through her.

He knew that she was thinking again about the horrors of last night and he said sharply,

"Forget them! Put them out of your mind and I suggest that you tell nobody, especially your uncle, what you have seen and heard."

Aspasia knew that the one person she would tell was Jerry, but certainly not Uncle Theophilus.

If she did so, he might think it his duty to remonstrate with the Duchess about her behaviour and that would be disastrous.

"You promise?" the Marquis insisted.

"I will say – nothing to my uncle," Aspasia promised. "He is a very saintly man and always thinks the best of everybody. I am sure that he has no idea of the wickedness that is taking place at Grimstone House."

"Them leave him happy in his ignorance," the Marquis said. "Most women talk too much, but I have the feeling that you are the exception."

"I would not – wish to speak of such – things," Aspasia said in a low voice, "and after you have been so kind I will – try to do as you – tell me."

The sun had risen over the horizon and now not only the sky but the whole world seemed to turn to gold and the Marquis was aware that with the light on Aspasia's hair it was as if he held a shaft of sunlight in his arms.

Never, he thought, had he seen hair of such a lovely colour and with his arm around her waist he realised how very light and slim she was. It was almost as if he held close to him some mythical nymph from the woods that they had just passed through.

And yet he knew that she was human enough to have been deeply shocked and frightened by what had occurred yesterday evening and it was something that should not have happened to any young girl let alone one of Aspasia's breeding and sensitivity.

'She will get over it,' the Marquis told himself.

At the same time he was afraid that it might be impossible.

They emerged between the trees of yet another wood and then ahead of them were the roofs of a grey stone building and beyond it the spire of a Church.

"Is this where you live?" the Marquis asked before Aspasia could point it out to him.

"Yes."

"I think it would be best if I don't take you to the door. I don't know what story you are going to tell your uncle and perhaps it will complicate things if he sees me."

"I don't think that Uncle Theophilus will be down to breakfast so early, but I will think of something to say before he does."

The Marquis guided his horse between the trees of a small orchard to stop at the edge of the untidy unkempt garden which was, however, ablaze with flowers.

"I will drop you here," he said. "Don't move, but hold the reins for me."

He put them into her hand, then dismounted and put up his arms to lift her to the ground.

As he did so, she looked down at him and, as the Marquis's grey eyes looked into hers, she had the strange feeling that they were speaking to each other without words.

Then very slowly, it seemed to her, he lifted her down from the saddle and held her for a moment against him before he set her free.

"Goodbye, Aspasia," he said and his voice was deep. "Take good care of yourself."

"Thank you – again," she replied and somehow it was hard to speak. "I shall – always remember your kindness – and how very wonderful you have been to – me."

Again his eyes were holding hers, but because she was shy and because she felt her heart beating in a very strange manner, she turned away and started to run over the unkempt lawn towards the house.

The Marquis saw her reach the front of it and then she disappeared behind some rosebushes.

He gave a sigh and it was only when he was riding back towards Grimstone House that he remembered Aspasia was still wearing his evening cloak.

'I wonder if she will return it to me,' he questioned and smiled.

Then he told himself that the sooner he could get away from the Duchess the better.

Equally he would have been foolish not to discuss with her the problem that had brought him to Grimstone House in the first place.

He wondered somewhat wryly if she would be disappointed when she found that he had no wish to accept another invitation to her cleverly calculated entertainment.

*

Aspasia let herself in through the side door where the lock had been broken for some time.

She realised as she did so that the house was very quiet, since, as it was still only a little past five o'clock, nobody was about.

She wanted to see Jerry, but there was no point in waking him.

She therefore went up to her own bedroom and only as she unclasped the cloak which the Marquis had given to her did she remember that she should have returned it to him.

'I can easily leave it at his house in Newmarket,' she reassured herself and thought that when she did so she would write him a letter of thanks and tell him once again how grateful she was.

She took off the white evening gown and wondered if the Duchess would ask for it to be sent back.

But for the moment she could think of nothing except that she was naked beneath it and it brought back to her the spectacle of the naked people on the stage in the dining room.

'I would like to burn this gown,' she thought. 'And hope that it would make me forget the whole of yesterday evening.'

At the same time she had no wish to forget the Marquis.

He was so handsome and so impressive. But he was also something else, something that she could not put into words.

Whatever it was she felt herself drawn to him in a very strange way and, when she had been close against him on his horse, it was almost as if she belonged to him.

'I am being imaginative,' Aspasia told herself.

But the feeling was there as she thought that it was just a sense of her security and now he had gone she would never know it again.

The whole world was suddenly dark.

'I am tired,' she thought, but knew that it was much more than that.

She put on her nightgown and climbed into the bed where she had slept ever since she had been too big for her cot and then she fell asleep thinking of the Marquis and wishing that she was still close to him.

*

Aspasia awoke to find that Jerry was standing by her bed looking down at her.

"Thank God you are back!" he exclaimed before she could speak. "I have been terrified ever since I received your message from the grooms."

Aspasia sat up.

"*You* had my message?" she asked. "I thought Martha would get it."

"Martha stayed the night with her relations," Jerry explained carelessly. "But what happened to you?"

Aspasia could not meet his eyes.

"I – hardly know how to – tell you," she answered, "and I am still – half-asleep."

"I tell you what I will do," Jerry said. "I will go downstairs and make some coffee. Put on your riding habit and after we have had breakfast I want you to come and see some fox cubs I have found. They are only just born and the prettiest little things imaginable, although they will play havoc with everybody's chickens when they grow older."

He went from the room as he spoke and Aspasia jumped out of bed.

Now she was back again in her own familiar surroundings and last night seemed just like a bad dream.

And yet, when she was relating it all to Jerry, the horror of it swept over her again.

They cooked their breakfast and, as it was too early for their uncle to require his, they ate it in the kitchen and Aspasia told her brother everything that had happened from the moment that she arrived at Grimstone House.

He listened first with an air of astonishment and then there was a frown between his eyes and his lips tightened as he realised the implications of many things that in her innocence she had not understood.

Only when she had finished and told him how she had slept peacefully beside the Marquis with a pillow between them on the bed did his fists, which he had subconsciously clenched, relax and he let out a deep sigh of relief.

"I can hardly believe it!"

"There is – something else I must tell you," Aspasia went on.

"What is that?"

"When I got up this morning, while the Marquis was in the bathroom I looked around the bedroom and what do you think I saw?"

"What did you see?" Jerry asked.

The most wonderful portrait of – you know who I am talking about – over the mantelpiece."

"I would like to see what he looked like."

"It would be very easy for you to do that."

"What do you mean?" Jerry asked.

"You can go and look in the mirror."

"Am I really so like him?"

"Exactly! The picture might have been of you except that it must have been painted when he was older."

As Aspasia spoke, she put her hand into the pocket of the jacket she was wearing and took out a miniature.

"I looked at this as soon as I came back this morning and I have always thought that this was very like you, but the portrait is, as Martha would say, 'the living image'."

"Well, there is nothing we can do about that," Jerry said. "All we can hope is that the Duchess never sees me."

"But – the grooms did who came – yesterday!"

"Well, there was nobody else to attend to them. Martha was not here and, although Uncle Theophilus was back, he was in the study."

"Do you think – they noticed you?"

He shook his head.

"No, of course not and I did not pay much attention to them. I just took your horse and put him in the stable."

"What were they like?"

"I really did not notice," Jerry smiled. "But I think one of the grooms was quite young and the other was an older man who led the second horse that the groom was to ride back on."

"I suppose it is – all right," Aspasia said doubtfully.

"After what you have been through last night, I should not think you need worry about anything more," Jerry said, "and for Heaven's sake, don't say anything to Uncle Theophilus."

"No, of course not," Aspasia agreed. "I will not tell him anything about the letter that came from the Duchess. There is no point in upsetting him."

As Jerry spoke, they heard their uncle coming down the stairs.

"I suppose you cleared the breakfast things from yesterday when you had supper," Aspasia said to her brother.

"Yes, that is right, but we left the supper plates without clearing them away."

Aspasia laughed.

"Well, go and do that now while I cook some eggs and bacon for Uncle Theophilus."

Jerry did as she told him and when she joined her uncle a little later he was reading a book.

"Good morning!" he murmured absent-mindedly.

She thought that it was so like him not to remember that she had been away last night.

"There are some very interesting references in this book," the Reverend Theophilus remarked, "on the influence of Plato on the Christian faith. I think you would enjoy reading it."

"I am sure I would," Aspasia replied, aware that Jerry's eyes were twinkling.

She gave him a little frown and said,

"Do eat your eggs and bacon while they are hot, Uncle Theophilus. What are you doing today? Jerry and I are going riding after breakfast."

"Good gracious me! It's a good thing you asked me that question," her uncle replied. "I have just remembered that I not only told Martha I would pick her up before noon, but I have also received a message that Mrs. Winthrop wishes to see me."

"Mrs. Winthrop!" Aspasia exclaimed. "Is she ill again?"

"I don't think she will last very long," the Reverend Theophilus informed her. "I therefore cannot refuse to visit her, but it will take me several hours to get there and back. As you well know, Bessie is very slow."

"But you will be back for supper," Aspasia said, "and please don't forget to collect Martha. We miss her."

"No, I will not forget," the Reverend Theophilus promised. "Jerry, will you put Bessie between the shafts for me? You are so much better at it than I am. I will go and get myself ready."

Aspasia knew that both she and Jerry were intensely relieved that her uncle had not been curious about her absence and that she was able to avoid telling him that she had been away for the night.

It took some time to take the gig round to the front door, find the special pair of spectacles that the Reverend Theophilus wished to take with him and pick some roses, which Aspasia felt that she should send to Mrs. Winthrop.

She was a kind old lady and, although not rich, was always prepared to support any special charity that the Vicar was interested in.

"Give Mrs. Winthrop our love," Aspasia urged him when at last he was ready to drive off, "and hurry back as quickly as you can."

The Reverend Theophilus merely smiled and, touching Bessie very lightly with his whip, set off down the drive.

"It is fortunate that Mrs. Winthrop and Plato are of more interest to Uncle Theophilus than you are," Jerry teased her.

"I am very very grateful to both of them," Aspasia laughed.

She tidied the house a little thinking that it would be a mistake for Martha to come back to unmade beds and a dining room table covered in dirty dishes.

Then they saddled their horses and set off across the fields.

They had quite a long way to ride to where Jerry had discovered the fox's lair in the depths of another wood where there was a sandpit amongst the trees.

There were no gamekeepers on this part of the estate and as they rode they saw magpies, jays, ferrets and stoats besides a large number of inquisitive little red squirrels.

It was hot and sunny and Aspasia, happy as she always was with Jerry, began to feel that everything that had happened last night was slipping away into the mists of oblivion.

She was, however, wondering as they returned home how she could explain to Martha the absence of her best gown and jacket and the fact that they had been replaced by a very fancy evening gown.

"We still have plenty of time to decide what you should and should not tell Martha," Jerry said, who as usual could read her thoughts.

"She will certainly ask me plenty of questions," Aspasia replied.

As they neared the Vicarage from a different direction from which she had come back this morning, Aspasia saw that there was a carriage standing outside the front door.

"I wonder who it can be!" she exclaimed pulling in her horse.

Jerry did the same and then the same question flashed through their minds like forked lightning.

Why should the Duchess have sent a carriage to the Vicarage?

It was closed and drawn by two horses. There was a coachman on the box, another man standing on the ground who looked like a footman and Aspasia thought that he was about to ring the bell.

Then she saw that the front door was open and it seemed to her strange that the Duchess's servants should have walked in.

But before she could say anything to Jerry a man appeared in the doorway and they both stiffened.

It was a man they knew well, in fact nobody could live on the Grimstone estate without knowing William Bollard by sight and reputation.

"What is he doing here?" Jerry asked beneath his breath.

They saw him say something to the footman and then go back into the house again.

They waited and then Aspasia gave a little gasp for she could see that Bollard and another man were in the room upstairs that was their uncle's.

The windows were open and the two men were moving about opening cupboards and drawers, pulling books from the bookshelves and scattering papers about.

"What are they doing?" Aspasia asked in a frightened whisper.

"They know!" Jerry exclaimed. "We had better get away! Come on, quickly."

He turned his horse as he spoke and went back through the trees that they had just emerged from.

"Where are we going?" Aspasia asked.

There was a little pause before Jerry replied,

"To Newmarket. The only person who can help us now is your Marquis."

*

The Marquis finished speaking and, standing with his back to the mantelpiece, waited for Charlie to comment.

"I can hardly believe it," Charlie said, "but I did warn you!"

"I wondered this morning," the Marquis added, "whether I should tell her exactly what I thought of her, but decided that there was no point in doing so."

"So you left the Duchess with the impression that you would return," Charlie remarked.

"I would not go so far as that," the Marquis answered. "I said firmly that I hoped that there would be no more unpleasant incidents on my boundary and that I would investigate the farmer's allegation that his fifteen-year-old daughter had disappeared."

"What did she say to that?"

"She merely remarked that girls of that age are inclined to go off with the first pedlar of pretty ribbons who takes their fancy and, since doubtless the girl would be found soon either in Newmarket or London, I would merely be wasting my time."

"In other words she appeared to brush it off?"

"Of course," the Marquis agreed, "and I believe that there is nothing that woman would not do! I am not surprised that she scares the whole countryside and I can only describe her as being like a hooded cobra!"

Charlie laughed.

"A very apt description. I am only surprised that you have come away unscathed."

"I only hope that the girl in the Vicarage is all right. She behaved with commendable courage, although fortunately she was too innocent to understand half of what was going on."

"Did you see any of the rest of the party before you left this morning?"

"None of them, thank goodness!" the Marquis replied. "I sent a message to the Duchess saying that as I wished to get home as soon as possible, I hoped that she would see me at her earliest convenience."

"So she appeared before anybody else."

"She seemed surprised that I was unaffected by the debauchery which I am certain will keep the others in bed until midday at least."

"I imagine that she herself did not drink very much," Charlie remarked.

"No, but she takes drugs."

"How do you know that?"

"The pupils of her eyes were dilated last night and I think the drugs she takes sharpen rather than sedate her brain. She only missed one point of what I was saying to her this morning, and never slipped up on the very plausible explanations she had for everything I asked her."

"She is a clever woman!"

"A *damnably* clever one!" the Marquis said violently. "I hope I never come in contact with her again!"

Charlie raised his eyebrows, but before he could say any more the butler announced luncheon and they went into the dining room.

As they finished an excellent but light meal, Charlie enquired,

"As you promised not to go back to London today, what do you propose we do?"

"I thought – " the Marquis began.

Before he could finish the sentence the door opened and the butler announced,

"Miss Aspasia Stanton has called on you, my Lord. I have shown her and a gentleman into the study. The young lady was most insistent on seeing your Lordship immediately although she has no appointment."

"That is all right," the Marquis said.

Charlie smiled.

"She has not taken long in following you. I wonder who she has brought with her?"

"Her uncle, I expect," the Marquis replied, "and this therefore means that I have to find him a Living."

Charlie laughed.

"That should not prove too difficult."

The Marquis walked towards the door.

"Come along, Charlie. I would like you to meet Miss Stanton."

"I have every intention of doing so after all I have heard about this young woman," Charlie replied with a grin.

The Marquis walked into the study and saw by the expression on Aspasia's face how glad she was to see him.

"Forgive me, please – forgive me for – troubling you," she began, "but my brother and I have nobody else we can turn to – and we are both very – frightened."

The Marquis took her hand in his and then looked towards the man standing behind her.

As he did so, the words he was about to speak died on his lips and he merely stared at Jerry in astonishment before he exclaimed,

"Good Heavens! I can hardly believe it!"

"I thought – you would – see the likeness," Aspasia murmured.

"Likeness?" the Marquis echoed. "And you say this is your brother?"

Jerry held out his hand.

"I am Jerome Stanton, my Lord, and I want to thank you for your kindness towards my sister. She has told me how you looked after her last night."

"It was certainly an unpleasant evening that your sister and I were involved in," the Marquis said, "but she never mentioned to me that you existed."

"Up to now neither Jerry nor I had ever seen the Duchess and for reasons that we can explain we had to keep Jerry hidden," Aspasia said. "But now she – knows! And it is – my fault."

There was a little sob in her voice as she said the last words and the Marquis looked at her in surprise.

Then he said,

"I feel you have a great deal to tell me, but first may I introduce my great friend, Charles Caversham, whom you may trust completely as you have trusted me."

"I am delighted to meet you, Miss Stanton," Charlie said. "The Marquis has been telling me how extremely brave you were in the most appalling circumstances."

"I was only brave because he was – kind enough to – look after me." Aspasia replied in a small voice. "And now we have to ask his help – again. There is – nobody else."

"I am only too willing to listen," the Marquis said, "but first of all I must ask you if you have had anything to eat. If not, my chef can easily produce some luncheon for you."

"No, it's all right, thank you very much," Aspasia answered. "Jerry insisted that we stopped at an inn on the way and had some bread and cheese. We thought that it would be embarrassing to arrive just as you were sitting down to luncheon."

"At least I can offer you a drink," the Marquis said. "I know already that Aspasia only likes lemonade, but I am sure, Stanton, you will not refuse a glass of champagne."

"Thank you very much, my Lord."

The Marquis poured out a glass of champagne for Jerry and some lemonade for Aspasia.

Charlie refused brandy and then on the Marquis's insistence they all sat down in the comfortable green leather armchairs.

As he joined them, he smiled at Aspasia as he said,

"Last night I told you to start at the beginning, but I know now that you must have left out a very important part of your story."

"It's a – secret we have never told – anybody," Aspasia answered, "but, as we rode here, Jerry and I decided that we would tell you the truth – because we know that you are the only – person who might be able to – help us."

"Then do so," the Marquis said as if he realised that was the whole point of the story.

Aspasia drew in her breath before she declared,

"The truth is that – Jerry is the – fourth Duke of Grimstone!"

CHAPTER FIVE

For a moment there was silence and then the Marquis asked,

"Why did you not tell me this when you were looking at the portrait of the Duke?"

Before Aspasia could reply Jerry said,

"It has been a secret that has been kept ever since we were born, my Lord, but when we returned home after riding this morning, we knew that the Duchess must have discovered my existence."

"How did you know that?" the Marquis enquired.

"We saw Bollard, the Duchess's Agent, and his men ransacking the house."

As he spoke, Aspasia gave a little cry.

"Uncle Theophilus! We have – forgotten about him. Supposing when he returns – "

She looked at Jerry with an expression of horror that the Marquis had seen in her eyes before.

"Yes, of course," Jerry responded. "I never thought of him. I must go back at once and prevent him from going home."

He started to rise to his feet, but the Marquis said quickly,

"Wait a minute! Let me get this clear. You think that your uncle is in some danger from this man Bollard? But why?"

"You have no idea what – he is like," Aspasia came in. "If people will not tell him what he wants to – know, he – tortures them!"

She saw the expression of incredulity on the Marquis's face and added,

"You don't believe me, but one man, Alfred Newlands, was – tortured to make him admit that he was poaching and he went mad. Then – afterwards he – killed himself!"

The terror vibrated in her voice and the Marquis said quietly,

"Tell me where your uncle is at this moment."

"He is visiting a Mrs. Winthrop, my Lord," Jerry answered. "She lives at Fetters Cross, which is about four miles out of Little Medlock."

"Wait here, I will see to it," the Marquis said and walked towards the door.

Aspasia looked at her brother.

"How could we have – forgotten that he might – hurt Uncle Theophilus?"

"Don't worry," Charlie said soothingly. "If there is one thing my friend the Marquis excels at, it is planning a campaign, which I see you have become and I assure you that there is no need for you to have any further fears about your uncle."

"I hope – you are – right," Aspasia stammered.

As if he wished to change the subject, Charlie went on,

"I never saw the third Duke, although I have heard a great deal about him. Is the likeness to your brother so striking that it would certainly be noticed by anyone who knew the Duke and not your brother?"

In answer to the question Aspasia took from the pocket of her riding jacket the miniature she carried.

"See for yourself!" she offered.

She held it out to Charlie who rose and took it from her.

He stared at it and then at Jerry.

"I have never seen such a remarkable likeness," he said. "Yet you two who are twins do not resemble each other."

"Mama said that I resembled the second Duchess," Aspasia said. "I believe that there is a portrait of her by Gainsborough, but I did not see it when I was at Grimstone House."

"How can the Duchess suddenly after all this time have guessed who you are?" Charlie enquired.

"It's all my – fault," Aspasia answered.

She told him how, when the Duchess had asked her to stay the night, she thought that she must let Jerry know that she was not returning home and sent a message to the Vicarage with two of her grooms.

"I expect the older groom remembered – our father," Jerry said ruminatingly.

There was a pause before he said the last two words because he and Aspasia had never referred to the Duke by any name, being always afraid that they might be overheard.

The Marquis came back into the room.

"I have sent my travelling chariot drawn by four horses," he said, "with a footman on the box who can handle a gun and my Agent, Jackson, who knows the way, to bring your uncle here."

"Oh, thank you – thank you!" Aspasia cried. "How can you be so kind and so – considerate."

She spoke with such feeling and with an expression in her eyes that made Charlie think that the Marquis had not only found a campaign to fight but had also already made an unexpected conquest.

Then he told himself that lovely and unusual though Aspasia was she was not likely to make much impression on a man who had had half the beauties of London Society ready to fall into his arms at the slightest encouragement.

"What I have to ask you now," the Marquis said briskly, "is if you have any evidence, apart from your undoubted resemblance, to substantiate the fact that you believe yourself to be the late Duke's son and heir."

"Of course we have," Aspasia replied, "and I think that is what Bollard was looking for."

"What is this evidence?"

"Mama's Marriage Certificate, a page of the Church Register in Little Medlock that she tore out with Uncle Theophilus's permission and a number of letters that our father wrote to her planning their secret marriage."

She paused for breath and the Marquis then asked,

"Where are these things?"

"Here in Newmarket in the Bank – Mama deposited them there for safety."

The Marquis frowned and then he said,

"I think before we waste any more time we should go and collect them just in case they fall into the wrong hands."

"You mean – that the Duchess – ?" Aspasia began.

"The Duchess is a very influential person in this part of the world," the Marquis said. "We had better go to the Bank."

He walked from the room and they heard him giving orders for a carriage to be brought round immediately.

They only had to wait a few minutes before it came to the door and they climbed into it to drive what was actually quite a short distance to the Bank in the main street of the small town.

The Marquis told Jerry what to say and when they entered the Bank he asked for the Manager.

Obviously impressed by their appearance the clerk showed them immediately into an office where a comparatively young man rose to greet them.

"I am Jerome Stanton," Jerry began, "and I and my sister, Miss Aspasia Stanton, wish you to hand over to us the sealed box that was deposited here seventeen years ago by my mother and which has been in your charge ever since."

There was an expression of surprise on the Manager's face and he said,

"This is very strange indeed, Mr. Stanton."

"What is?" Jerry asked.

"That you should arrive at this particular moment."

"I don't understand."

"Well, sir, a quarter of an hour ago a gentleman arrived here with a letter from Her Grace the Duchess of Grimstone asking me for any documents deposited by Mrs. Stanton."

"You did not give them to her?" Aspasia asked before anybody else could speak.

"I was in fact worried about what to do," the Manager replied, "because I understood that the instructions given at the time by Mrs. Stanton were that the box could be handed over only to her children if they applied for it jointly."

"Then it is still here?" Jerry asked.

"The gentleman representing Her Grace was very persistent and not liking to refuse such an important client, I have asked him to wait in another room while I sent for the last Manager, who recently retired but lives in the town, to ask his advice."

Aspasia gave an audible sigh.

"Then the box is – here."

"Yes, Miss Stanton, but I do not know that."

Before he could say anything more the Marquis intervened.

"I am the Marquis of Thame," he said. "I think perhaps you know me by name."

"Yes, indeed, my Lord," the Manager said eagerly, "and may I say we are very gratified that you are one of our patrons."

"Then as your Patron," the Marquis said firmly, "I advise you to carry out your instructions to the letter and hand over to Mr. Jerome Stanton and Miss Aspasia Stanton, both of whom I can vouch for, the box that was deposited by their mother and which in no circumstances should be given to any other person, however important their credentials might appear to be."

The Manager was obviously impressed and at the same time somewhat disturbed by the sarcastic tone in which the Marquis referred indirectly to the Duchess.

"I will fetch the box at once, my Lord," he said. "And, please, Miss Stanton, will you take a seat?"

Aspasia did not sit, but merely waited apprehensively until the Manager returned, pink in the face because he had been hurrying, with a small square box in his hand that was sealed in several places.

He put it down on the desk and produced a form.

"Will you, Miss Stanton, and your brother, be kind enough to sign this form?" he asked. "And I should be much obliged, my Lord, in case there are any difficulties with Her Grace, if you would sign it too."

"Certainly," the Marquis agreed at once.

When they drove away with Jerry carrying the precious box tightly under one arm, Aspasia turned to the Marquis,

"How could you have – guessed that the Duchess would try to obtain the documents? How could you have been so – clever as to get us here – just in time?"

"I am convinced that the Duchess will stop at nothing to make certain that she keeps her title and her position as your father's heiress," the Marquis said, "and that is why I have a plan, which must be put into operation immediately!"

When they walked into the house, Aspasia moved towards the room where they had been sitting earlier, but the Marquis stayed behind and they could hear his voice in the hall giving orders to the servants, although they could not hear what he said.

Then he joined them closing the door firmly behind him and walking to stand in front of the mantelpiece as he said,

"Now listen to me. This is very important. You, Stanton, will leave within fifteen minutes for London with my friend, Charlie Caversham."

The Marquis looked at Charlie as he spoke almost as if he expected him to protest, but there was a twinkle in Charlie's eyes and a faint smile on his lips so the Marquis went on,

"You, Charlie, will drive my chestnuts and the phaeton, which is the fastest vehicle I have. You will have a groom with you and you will be accompanied by four outriders, one of whom will be Stanton."

They all stared at the Marquis and even Charlie seemed surprised.

"I am taking no chances," the Marquis went on. "I have a feeling that the Duchess will by this time realise that you have not returned to the Vicarage and be desperate to stop you from reaching London. She may anticipate that you will petition the Prince Regent."

"Shall I do that?" Jerry asked.

The Marquis shook his head.

"No. It is much too soon and far too dangerous for you to go anywhere where you could be eliminated by having what would be undoubtedly called an 'unfortunate accident'."

"Then what shall I do when we reach London?" Jerry enquired.

"You and Charlie will go straight to Berkeley Square where my second valet will fit you out with any clothes you require," the Marquis replied. "We are about the same size and I daresay you will not object at this particular moment to wearing a second hand wardrobe."

Intent though she was on listening to what the Marquis was saying, Aspasia could not help a glance at Jerry, which revealed the glint in his eye that she knew was one of excitement.

He had always longed to wear expensive and well-cut clothes as most of his friends did and she knew that, tense and apprehensive though they were, Jerry would not have missed seeing that the Marquis was the epitome of elegance and it would be impossible for any man to look better dressed.

"You will spend as little time as possible in Berkeley Square," the Marquis was saying, "and with a change of horses you will set off immediately for Dover."

"Dover!" Charlie exclaimed. "But by that time it will be growing dark."

"There is a moon tonight," the Marquis replied, "and if you feel tired you will have plenty of time to rest when you are aboard my yacht."

Charlie gave a laugh.

"Mervyn, I congratulate you! As usual you have come up with a plan which will certainly take the enemy by surprise."

"That is what I hope. A courier will, of course, be ahead of you and the moment you are aboard the Captain will be ready to sail."

"And where are we to go? Have you also decided that?"

"Of course!" the Marquis answered. "You will sail down the South Coast of England. To every Port of call, Newhaven, Portsmouth, Exmouth, Plymouth, I will send you news of what is happening and let you know if it is safe for you to return."

"And if it is not?"

"Then you can take a trip to the Mediterranean or any other place that takes your fancy."

"I can only say that I am thrilled, my Lord," Jerry exclaimed. "If there is one thing I have always wanted to do, it is to go to sea in a private yacht!"

"All you have to do is to get safely to Dover," the Marquis said. "I suggest now that you go and change. My valet will have the right clothes waiting for you."

Jerry rose to his feet.

"I just don't know how to thank you, my Lord."

"You can thank me by keeping alive," the Marquis said, "until I have proved your claim in the House of Lords."

Aspasia made a little sound of delight.

Jerry looked at her and then with an obvious but unspoken question at the Marquis.

"You can leave your sister with me," the Marquis assured him. "I will see that she comes to no harm and will take the same precautions where she is concerned that I have taken for you."

He would not listen to Jerry's grateful thanks, but hurried him up the stairs and along a passage into a room at the end of it.

A short while later when the Marquis escorted Aspasia there she found that her brother was almost unrecognisable.

He was wearing tight-fitting white breeches, a green coat with yellow collar and cuffs and crested silver buttons, which she recognised as the Marquis's livery.

On Jerry's head was a white wig, tied at the back of the neck with a black bow and over it was a black velvet peaked cap.

"Oh, Jerry, you look fantastic!" Aspasia exclaimed.

"It's rather a tight fit, miss," the valet remarked.

"You can change back into your own clothes when you are well away from Newmarket," the Marquis said, "but don't waste time. For all we know the Duchess may already have sent some of her assassins to London. If they ride-cross country, they will be quicker than you are by road."

"I will not waste a second more than is necessary, my Lord," Jerry promised. "Goodbye, Aspasia."

She put her arms around her brother's neck and kissed him.

"I shall be praying that you will be – all right," she sighed, "and I have a feeling that now that the Marquis is helping us everything in the future is going to be – very very different."

"I am sure of it," Jerry said confidently, "and thank you again, my Lord."

They shook hands and, as Jenkins took him away, the Marquis turned to Aspasia,

"If anybody is watching my friend leave, they will not expect you to notice the servants who accompany him."

"No, of course not," Aspasia agreed.

They went downstairs and found Charlie already in the hall and the Marquis talked to him in front of the footmen as if he was just leaving in the ordinary way.

"I will join you tomorrow, Charlie," he said. "Then we will decide about going to Thame, but I am afraid that His Royal Highness will expect us to be in attendance on him for a day or so at any rate."

"I am sure he will," Charlie grinned.

The door was open and they saw a phaeton outside, drawn by a perfectly matched team of superlative horseflesh.

"Be careful how you handle them," the Marquis warned, "and if you break my record I shall be annoyed!"

"I shall certainly do my best," Charlie laughed. "Goodbye, Mervyn, I have enjoyed my visit and look forward to seeing you tomorrow."

"I will let you know what time to expect me," the Marquis replied.

Charlie held out his hand to Aspasia.

"Goodbye, Miss Stanton. It has been a great pleasure to meet you."

As she curtseyed, he said in a low voice that only she could hear,

"Don't worry, I will look after him for you."

Aspasia gave him a little smile that he thought to himself was very lovely.

Then he climbed into the phaeton and, as he drove off, the four outriders who had been waiting a little way behind moved forward to ride on the grass verge protectively, two on each side of the vehicle.

Aspasia watched until her brother was out of sight and sent a little prayer after him.

The Marquis walked away as if he was not particularly interested in the departing cavalcade and was anxious to return to the comfort of his sitting room.

She joined him feeling shy because they were alone and he indicated a chair as he said,

"Now I want to hear your story from the beginning."

"Yes – of course," Aspasia replied.

She had taken off her bonnet and her hair seemed like a flaming halo around her head as she said,

"It seems strange to be able to talk about – my father after all these – years."

"I don't at all understand why it had to be kept a secret," the Marquis remarked.

"When my grandfather died – " Aspasia began.

"What was his name?" the Marquis interrupted.

"General Sir Alexander Stanton. He was knighted when he commanded the Coldstream Guards."

"A very fine Regiment," the Marquis commented.

"My grandfather had three children," Aspasia went on, "his eldest son also served in the Brigade and was killed in the War. His second son was Uncle Theophilus and he had always wanted to go into the Church. I think it was because it gave him a chance to go to Oxford University as a Scholar – which was really the only thing that interested him."

Aspasia paused and the Marquis said as if he were prompting her,

"And your mother?"

"My mother was much younger than Uncle Theophilus and when she grew up she spent three years of her life nursing my grandfather until he died. When he did – she came to the Vicarage at Little Medlock."

"Where I presume she met your father?" the Marquis questioned.

"They met almost as soon as she arrived," Aspasia answered. "His wife had just died after a very long illness and during the last year she had been in a coma and so was unable to recognise anybody."

"What year was this?" the Marquis enquired.

"The end of 1799 and it was Christmas. Mama was decorating the Church when the Duke came to see Uncle Theophilus about a plaque he wished to erect in memory of his wife."

"So they met in Church," the Marquis said with a smile.

"Mama said that she fell in love with the Duke the moment he walked down the aisle and he told her later that she was – so beautiful that he thought she was an angel and not a human being."

"What happened?" the Marquis asked.

"The Duke asked Mama to marry him and told her that he could not possibly wait for the year of mourning that was expected of a widower and especially of somebody in his position. That is why Uncle Theophilus married them secretly. Then the Duke took Mama away to a house he owned in Cornwall."

"The Duke must have been much older than your mother."

"Very much older, but Mama always said, 'love is ageless'."

Aspasia gave a little sigh.

"Mama told me that they were so happy that it was like being in Heaven and whatever happened afterwards – she had that to remember all her life."

"What did happen?" the Marquis asked.

"Although the Duke was much older than Mama, she always said that he seemed like a young man and because they were so happy he behaved like one. They rode together, they swam in the sea – and he never seemed tired."

The Marquis had calculated that the Duke must have been about sixty-five at the time, but Aspasia's description of him fitted with what he had already heard about him.

"They were idyllically happy," Aspasia went on, "and Mama said that every day they grew more and more in love. Then came – tragedy."

"What happened?" the Marquis asked.

"They were sitting by the sea when they saw a young man struggling in the water. There were undercurrents that were dangerous and he was obviously not a strong swimmer. He was shouting for help and, of course, the Duke went to his assistance."

"He saved him?"

"He saved him, but for no reason Mama could understand, except that they had only just had luncheon, the Duke got cramp as he was guiding the man into safer waters and – he was drowned."

"That was certainly a tragedy," the Marquis agreed.

"It was terrible for Mama. She had to watch the Duke being swept away – and there was nothing she could do to help him."

"Why did she not announce that they were married?" the Marquis asked.

"Because Mama thought that, as the Duke was so important, people would criticise him for having married secretly so soon after his wife's death. So she decided to say nothing and – came back to the Vicarage alone."

"But surely the servants must have known?"

"The Duke had taken with them to Cornwall only those he could trust. They would never without his permission have betrayed the fact that he had remarried."

"So his daughter had no idea of what had happened."

"None at all. After her mother died she had gone to Scotland to stay with some friends in Edinburgh. She returned only just in time for her father's funeral. His body was recovered from the sea and he was taken home to lie in state as was usual when a Duke of Grimstone died."

Aspasia paused for a moment and then she said,

"It was only when the funeral was over and the Duchess had taken charge of everything that Mama found – that she was going to have a baby."

"But still she kept her secret?"

"She was desperately unhappy and she was also still thinking of the Duke's reputation, so she decided to say nothing until later. Then it was – too late."

"What do you mean by that?"

"Mama was ill for some time after we were born, I think because we were twins and also because she was – so unhappy."

"I can understand that."

"Then when she was stronger and she thought that for Jerry's sake she should announce that the Duke had a son, she was frightened."

"By the Duchess?"

"From the moment her father was no longer there the Duchess began to behave in a very autocratic manner to the people on the estate and her agent, Bollard, did the most cruel and wicked things in her name."

"Did you mean it when you said that he actually tortured people?"

"Yes, and he also when it suited him, turned families out of their cottages and trumped up charges against anybody he disliked to the Magistrates. Two men were transported on what Mama was sure was 'false evidence'."

Aspasia lowered her voice as if she was still frightened as she added,

"One man who refused to leave the cottage that he had lived in for years had his doors and windows boarded up. He was inside – and he died of – starvation."

"I can hardly believe that such things could actually happen!" the Marquis exclaimed.

"You can understand that Mama was frightened for us. We had nobody to protect us – and very little money."

"The Duke had not given her any?"

"He had intended to settle a lot of money on herm – but he naturally had no idea that he was going to die so soon after they were married and, when he did die, all she had was the money he had given her to buy a trousseau."

Aspasia gave a little sigh before she continued,

"Mama had some lovely jewels that the Duke had bought her before they had married, but she sold these to pay for Jerry's school fees."

Aspasia clasped her hands together as she said,

"That money has nearly all – gone, so you can understand now why it is so terribly – important for Uncle Theophilus not to have to leave the Parish and lose his stipend."

"There is no need for you to worry about that," the Marquis said. "I have already told you that I will look after your uncle and, of course, you and Jerry until he can claim his inheritance."

"Do you really – think he will be – able to do so?"

"I am certain of it," the Marquis smiled. "And now let us open this precious box."

"Yes – of course – but it terrifies me to think how – nearly we lost it!"

"But fortunately it is in our hands," the Marquis said reassuringly, "and I only hope that we will find everything inside exactly as you described."

He began to break the seals on the box.

"Mama always believed and prayed that one day Jerry would become the Duke," Aspasia said, "but you can understand that as the years went by things became worse instead of better as the reputation of the Duchess became more notorious and Bollard had more and more power."

The Marquis thought that she was confirming everything that Jackson had told him about the situation on the Grimstone estate. Even so he found it hard to believe such outrage could happen and nobody be prepared to do anything about it.

However, he supposed that the Duchess had her own methods of keeping the Chief Constable, the High Sheriff and anybody else of local importance from interfering.

As he saw the Marriage Certificate and the Church Register and read the letters that the Duke had written to Elizabeth Stanton, it was obvious that Jerry would have no difficulty in proving his claim.

At the same time he told himself that it would be a great mistake to underestimate the efforts that the Duchess would make to prevent this from happening.

He did not, however, wish to frighten Aspasia and, as he put the papers back into the box, he said,

"I am going to place this in a safe for the night, not the main safe, which is in a part of the house which could be broken into, but one that is in my bedroom and known only to myself and my valet."

"You don't think that – anybody would come here – tonight to try to steal it?" Aspasia asked and there was a distinctly nervous tremor in her voice.

"I think it very unlikely that the Duchess would do anything foolhardy," the Marquis observed. "She will know when her emissary returns from the Bank that we have the box but her main concern for the moment will be Jerry. After all the box would be quite useless if he was dead."

Aspasia gave a little cry of horror.

Then she said,

"Perhaps it would be – wisest to promise once and for all that we will continue to keep silence. It will be no use Jerry being a Duke if he is always to be – afraid of being killed in some – way or another. We have been very happy – just as we are."

"I am sure you have," the Marquis smiled.

He thought that most women in Aspasia's place would risk almost anything for her brother to be a Duke.

But he could understand looking at Aspasia that her mother had been no less sensitive than she was, for only a very sensitive woman could have kept such an important marriage secret solely to protect her husband's reputation.

"Did you not mind when you knew that your mother was prepared to remain in obscurity?" he asked. "You must have found your life in Little Medlock extremely restricted."

"We were very very happy when Mama was alive," Aspasia answered, "and I am happy when I am with Jerry. After all we are twins."

"I think that both you and Jerry deserve much more than to live under a cloud for the rest of your lives."

"At least we are – alive and it would be no use being – grand if we had always to be – afraid."

The Marquis knew that she was thinking of how afraid she had been last night and so he said,

"You must somehow contrive to forget what happened."

"Do you think – Jerry and your friend will – reach London safely?" Aspasia asked.

"I am sure of it," the Marquis said firmly. "Three of my best men are with them, all of whom can use a pistol very efficiently. They are used to coping with highwaymen who I assure you can be very tiresome on the roads that are frequented by rich racegoers."

"Jerry is – a good shot as well."

"He has a pistol with him," the Marquis replied, "so stop worrying, Aspasia, and let me show you some of my pictures. I know you would like to see them."

He saw her eyes light up.

"Can we – really?"

"I will take you on a tour of inspection," he answered, "starting in this room."

They went round the house together and Aspasia was thrilled and delighted by the pictures, which were mostly of sporting subjects.

There was so much to see and so many questions that she wanted to ask that she was quite surprised when it was teatime.

She was pouring from a very fine silver teapot made by a Master craftsman in the fifteenth century, when the door was opened.

"The Reverend Theophilus Stanton, my Lord," the butler announced.

Aspasia gave a cry of joy and jumped up to kiss her uncle.

"Oh, Uncle Theophilus! You are here! I am – so glad to see you."

"I am glad you are all right, my dear, but whatever is happening?"

The Reverend Theophilus, the Marquis noticed, was a good-looking man. Although he had the expression and the gait of a scholar who was always poring over books, there was, he was to find later, a twinkle in his eyes when his sense of humour was aroused.

Now, however, he was only looking anxious as he held out his hand to the Marquis and said,

"You were kind enough to send your carriage for me, my Lord, and your Agent has been relating to me some very unpleasant incidents that have occurred on the borders of your estate and the one we live in. But I cannot believe that that is the reason why you have such urgent need of my company."

"No, it is a little more complicated than that," the Marquis replied.

Aspasia asked her uncle to sit down and while she poured him out a cup of tea she told him that the Duchess had learned of Jerry's identity.

The Reverend Theophilus looked worried.

"How could Her Grace have found out?"

Aspasia chose her words with care.

"One of her grooms called yesterday with a note for you, Uncle Theophilus, and unfortunately he saw Jerry and he must have noticed the striking likeness he has to our – father."

The Reverend Theophilus sighed.

"I was afraid something like this might happen sooner or later, since Jerry is so exactly like his father. It would be impossible for anybody who knew the Duke not to notice the resemblance."

"Now it has been noticed," the Marquis said, "we have to prove that Jerry is the rightful heir to the title and, because I feel that the most important thing is that he should be safe while negotiations take place, I have sent him away."

He explained briefly where Jerry was and the Reverend Theophilus, although slightly bewildered by what had happened, accepted it philosophically.

"I was sure it was a secret we could not keep for ever," he said at length, "but I am afraid there will be a great deal of unpleasantness when the Duchess learns of it."

"She has learned of it," the Marquis replied, "and the reason why Aspasia and her brother came to me for my help was that they saw Bollard and some of his men ransacking your bedroom."

"Good gracious!" the Reverend Theophilus exclaimed and then added in a more serious tone, "I presume they were looking for evidence of a marriage."

"Yes," the Marquis agreed, "but fortunately I have it safely here and I am going to take it upstairs now and put it away in a safe."

He rose as he spoke and Aspasia looked at her uncle.

"Martha is upset as you can imagine," he said. "I think, my dear, you should go and talk to her and reassure her that everything will be all right."

"I hope it will be," Aspasia said in a low voice.

Talking to Martha, Aspasia managed to hide from her that she had been to Grimstone House and what she had found there.

Instead she told Martha that the letter, which had been brought by a groom to the Vicarage, had been to dismiss her uncle from the Parish.

"I've never heard anythin' so wicked in all my life!" Martha cried. "Her Grace's a monster and there's no two ways about it. If you asks me, Miss Aspasia, it would be a good thing if we could all go away from Little Medlock and never come back!"

"I think that is what we are – going to – do," Aspasia murmured.

"Well, I for one shan't cry any tears at leavin' it," Martha said tartly. "And now perhaps you'll tell me what you are goin' to wear for dinner if you've come here in nothin' but your ridin' habit!"

"I certainly will not look very smart," Aspasia agreed, "but there is nothing I can do about it."

She did, however, feel rather embarrassed when she had to go downstairs wearing her riding skirt and the muslin blouse that she wore with it.

She was very conscious that her skirt was almost threadbare and, although the blouse was pretty, it certainly did not compare with the elaborate white evening gown that she had worn last night.

Martha had brushed her hair and it shone with red lights like the setting sun and the Marquis found it impossible to look at anything else as she came into the drawing room before dinner and the light from the candles seemed to make her hair gleam with a light of its own.

As he set out to make himself extremely agreeable both to the Reverend Theophilus and to Aspasia, dinner was a meal when they laughed a great deal while they enjoyed superlative food and excellent wine.

When it was over, the Marquis was aware that, after the dramatics of last night and the fears and apprehensions she had gone through today, Aspasia was very tired.

"I suggest you go to bed," he said. "We shall be leaving early tomorrow morning and I want you to have a proper rest."

"I – do feel a little – sleepy," Aspasia confessed.

"Then go to sleep," he urged, "and don't worry about anything. Although I feel certain that you will not be disturbed tonight, there will be extra nightwatchmen on duty with instructions to wake me if anything unusual occurs."

"I am sure you need to sleep too," Aspasia suggested.

She smiled at him quite naturally as she was thinking of how early they had both risen.

Then, as she met his eyes, she remembered how they had slept together in the same bed and she blushed.

She said 'goodnight' to her uncle and went upstairs to Martha who was waiting to help her undress.

"I've found a nightgown for you," she said, "but it's not what I considers very respectable."

Aspasia looked at it with interest.

"Apparently it was left behind by one of his Lordship's guests," Martha explained, "Lady somebody or other, I can't remember her name, but the housemaids tell me she was a great beauty. That's as may be, but her nightgown's nothin' but a bit of lawn and lace!"

Actually Aspasia thought that the nightgown was very pretty and she wished that she could have worn it last night when the Marquis was with her.

Then she was surprised at herself for even thinking such a thing and quickly climbed into bed.

"If you want me," Martha was saying, "pull the bell that rings in the housemaids' room. I'll arrange for one of them to fetch me."

"I am sure I shall not need anything," Aspasia replied. "Goodnight, Martha, and it is lovely to be here. I should feel very frightened if we were at home now."

She knew that Martha wanted to agree with her, but thought it best to say nothing and merely blew out the candles.

"Goodnight, God bless you," she said.

Then Aspasia was alone.

She fell asleep instantly and a long time later when she was having a complicated dream in which she was running away from the Duchess who was pursuing her with a glass of wine in her hand she awoke with a start.

The room was in darkness, but there was a silver streak of light on either side of the curtain, and she knew that the moon must be high in the sky.

She thought of Jerry and Mr. Caversham driving towards Dover and reckoned that, if they drove as fast as the Prince Regent had done on his record drive when he was Prince of Wales, they would soon be there.

'I wish I could be with them,' she thought, thinking what fun it would be to be on a yacht.

Then, as she thought about it, she was quite certain that she would rather be with the Marquis. He was so interesting and he had made her laugh when he was taking her round the house to view his pictures.

'It must have been boring for him,' she thought with a little sigh, 'but very very exciting for me.'

She closed her eyes thinking that she would recall all over again what he had said to her and then make sure that she never forgot anything.

Then she heard a slight sound.

It was very slight and yet it was undoubtedly a sound that was not part of the night.

She listened and suddenly she was afraid.

All the fears that had swept over her when she saw Bollard ransacking her uncle's bedroom came back and with them the fear that she had felt last night from the evil that emanated from the Duchess and Mrs. Fielding.

Then came a thousand other fears that had accumulated over the years to hang over them all like a menacing cloud that she could never escape from.

Hardly realising what she was doing, yet feeling that she must reassure herself that here in the Marquis's house she was safe, she slipped out of bed and crept towards the window.

She drew the curtains aside to peep through them.

The moonlight was blinding and her bedroom, which looked out onto the front of the house, had a view of the drive, which was bordered by high rhododendron bushes and trees.

Everything seemed quite quiet.

Then down the drive in the shadows she saw something that held her attention.

For a moment it was difficult to see what it was. Then she realised that it was the back of a carriage.

Her heart gave a frightened leap and for the first time she looked down.

There was a small balcony beneath her window. It was merely part of the ornamentation of the house and there was no room for anybody to do anything more than just stand on it.

It had a grey stone balustrade and in the centre of it she saw a rope that was moving.

For a moment her brain seemed to stop functioning and she could not think and certainly could not imagine what the rope was doing there.

Then it suddenly struck her that it was a rope that a man could climb up and into her room.

She did not wait to see anymore.

She only knew that the carriage and the rope told her what was happening and she was filled with a wild uncontrollable fear that drove her to seek the only person who could save her.

She moved backwards and ran silently across the thick carpet and opened the door of her bedroom.

Then she was speeding down the passage to the room at the far end where she had said 'goodbye' to Jerry.

She did not stop to think or remember the nightwatchmen on duty.

She pulled open the door of the Marquis's bedroom and finding it impossible to speak, for no sound would come from her throat, she merely tore towards the bed where she knew he would be lying to fling herself against him.

*

The Marquis was not asleep because he found that he had so much to think about that he was not at all tired.

He had actually been sitting up against his pillows making notes on a pad that was by his bed so that he would not forget all the things he had to do in the morning.

He had just put the pad down and blown out the candles, but was still in a sitting position looking across the room at the moonlight that was streaming through an uncurtained window.

He too had been thinking of Charlie and Jerry journeying towards Dover and wishing in a way he could be with them.

The danger of knowing that they might be pursued would be exciting, but his yacht waiting for them in the Harbour would constitute a place of safety where it would be almost impossible for the enemy to encroach.

Meanwhile, the Marquis thought, with a smile of satisfaction, everything was going according to plan, but it was always a mistake to be optimistic until one had actually won the battle.

He was just thinking that he should throw aside his pillows to lie down and try to sleep when the door of his room burst open.

The next minute someone small and terrified was clinging to him and he could feel her body trembling against his.

As his arms went round Aspasia, she gasped,

"Th-they are – there outside – my window, they – have come to take me – away, oh – save me – *save me!*"

CHAPTER SIX

For a moment the Marquis could hardly believe what Aspasia was saying as she cried in a frantic tone,

"Bollard will – torture me to – tell him – where Jerry is. I cannot – bear it!"

The Marquis lifted her away from him and onto the bed.

Then, as he stepped onto the floor, he said,

"No one will hurt you. Stay here and I will lock you in. Try not to be afraid."

The calm way he spoke checked Aspasia's gasping cries for a moment. Then, as he put on a long dark robe and reached for the loaded pistol that was beside his bed, she said,

"Be – c-careful. Please – be careful. Supposing they – hurt you?"

"I shall be all right," the Marquis said. "Get under the bedclothes and keep warm until I return."

He went from the room as he spoke and she heard the key turn in the lock.

Then, because she wanted to hide, she did as he said and slipped into the bed and pulled the bedclothes over her head.

The Marquis walked quickly down the passage.

He considered whether he should call the nightwatchmen, but then decided he had no wish to let the intruders escape before he had a chance to deal with them.

Aspasia's door was open and the Marquis moved silently towards the window, pulling the curtain only a few inches aside so that he could peep through it.

He saw, as Aspasia had, the back of the carriage in the shadows and the rope round the balustrade.

It was still moving and he was aware that it had been thrown skilfully from the ground with a well-muffled hook on the end of it, to catch into the top of the balustrade, which made it easy for an athletic man to climb.

At the window that opened onto the balcony the Marquis was in a position where he could see through the curtain and be directly opposite the rope on the balustrade.

Everything was very quiet and he was aware that the man or men who were menacing Aspasia were very experienced at their job.

He wondered if they were in fact anticipating that this bedroom which a light shone from might contain Jerry, as it was he they wished to assassinate.

At the same time it seemed feasible that an alternative was to take away Aspasia and, as she had said, torture her into telling them where they could find her brother.

The Marquis waited.

He had very acute hearing and he was sure now as the rope tightened that the man was gradually approaching the balcony from the ground.

It was not a very long ascent. Actually he had to admit that he had not calculated when planning his defence of the house that the Duchess's men would be so daring as to enter from the first floor.

A hand appeared to grasp the top of the balustrade, then another and a moment later the Marquis peeping through only the merest crack in the curtain could see a man's face who he was certain was Bollard.

The description he had been given by Jackson fitted him exactly and he could not help thinking that it was quite an achievement for a man who was over forty to climb so silently.

Then, as the intruder flung his leg over the balustrade, the Marquis acted.

With the unerring aim of a crack shot he fired to hit Bollard exactly on the kneecap, which he was aware would not only be crippling but also extremely painful.

The explosion of the gun seemed to echo through the still air.

With a shriek Bollard tumbled backwards and crashed onto the ground below.

The Marquis pulled back the curtain to step out onto the balcony.

First he saw two men running in the direction of the carriage and making no effort to go to the assistance of their fallen accomplice.

The fall had not however rendered Bollard unconscious and he pulled himself up onto his elbow to yell after them,

"Help me, damn you! For God's sake, *help* me!"

The men went on running and, as the Marquis thought that by this time the nightwatchmen would have heard the shot and come hurrying from the house, he saw a horse emerge from the shadows.

At first he thought that it was being ridden by a slim young man. Then in the moonlight he could see the rider's face quite clearly and realised with astonishment that it was the Duchess.

She pulled her horse to a standstill and looking down at the man on the ground she said venomously,

"You blundering fool, you have failed! Now you will be taken away for questioning and that is something I cannot allow."

As she spoke, she pulled a pistol from a holster in her saddle and as she did so Bollard, as he sensed what she was about to do, took a pistol from the pocket of his coat.

It was just a question of who was the quicker and even as Bollard pulled the trigger of his weapon the Duchess's finger tightened on hers.

Two explosions rang out almost simultaneously and for a moment the watching Marquis thought that they had both missed.

Then, as the Duchess's horse reared up in fright and threw her, he realised from the way that she fell to the ground that she was dead.

By the time the Marquis was downstairs and had joined the nightwatchmen who were hurrying out of the house after unlocking the doors, he found that both the Duchess and Bollard were dead while there was no sign of the other men who had accompanied them.

With his usual quickness of mind the Marquis decided that the last thing he wanted was an enquiry as to why the Duchess and Bollard were both found dead outside his house.

Instead he had them loaded into the back of a brake and sent them back to the Grimstone Estate with two men who had been in his service for a long time and whom he could trust implicitly.

He ordered that the two bodies should be set down near Bollard's house and as both men knew where it was he calculated that it would not be difficult for them to unload the corpses and be back in Newmarket well before it was dawn.

He then told the nightwatchmen who again were men he could trust to forget everything they had seen and speak of it to nobody.

He looked out over a quiet moonlit garden and, thinking that it was difficult to realise what had happened so quickly and so unexpectedly, he went upstairs to Aspasia.

There had been no sign from the Reverend Theophilus and the Marquis was certain that being slightly deaf he had not heard the three shots. Fortunately the servant's bedrooms all looked out onto the other side of the house.

As he walked up the stairs from the hall, he thought that nothing could have worked out better from everybody's point of view.

It would be a mistake for Jerry on starting his new life as the Duke of Grimstone to have been in any way involved even indirectly with the death of the Duchess.

For Aspasia too a new world was opening up before her that the shadows of the past must not encroach on.

The Marquis unlocked the door of his bedroom and he had only just come inside before there was a cry that he had somehow expected.

Aspasia rose from the bed and ran across the room and flung herself against him.

"W-what has – happened? Why have you – been so long? I – heard shots and was afraid – desperately afraid – you might have been – killed!"

The tremor on the last words told the Marquis how much she had suffered and he put his arm around her as he said gently,

"It's all over. You need not be upset any longer. The Duchess is dead!"

"D-dead?"

Aspasia raised her head from his shoulder and he could see in the moonlight coming through the window the astonishment in her eyes.

"I am going to tell you what happened," the Marquis said, "then we will never speak of it again because the way they died *must* be kept a secret."

He drew her as he spoke towards the bed and, as he sat down on it with his arm around her, he realised how very little she was wearing and that she was still trembling, although not as violently as when she had first come to him in terror.

"You are cold," he said, "and I suggest while I tell you what has happened you get into bed and keep warm."

Like a child Aspasia obeyed him and, when she was sitting up against the pillows, she pulled the sheets modestly over her shoulders and said,

"Tell me – please – tell me what has happened – I was so – frightened for you."

"And for yourself," the Marquis said with a smile.

"And for Jerry and Uncle Theophilus," Aspasia added. "There is only – you to – protect us."

"Which I have done very successfully," the Marquis said with a note of satisfaction in his voice.

"Is it true – really true that the Duchess is – dead?"

"She is dead and therefore she can never hurt you again," the Marquis answered. "Now Jerry can claim his rightful place and everything in the future will be very different for both of you."

"If it is – then it is all – due to you," Aspasia said, "and how can we – ever thank you?"

She put out her hand as she spoke and the Marquis had the idea that it was not so much an expression of gratitude but because she wished to hold onto him and believe what he was telling her was the truth.

Very briefly, in a few words, he told her how he had shot Bollard in the knee, how the man had fallen to the ground and how the Duchess had shot him to prevent him from being questioned but that he had shot her simultaneously.

He spoke quietly. At the same time he was aware of the horror that was reflected in Aspasia's eyes as her fingers tightened on his.

"They cannot hurt you anymore," he finished.

"It is still a – terrible way to die – without having time to pray for – forgiveness."

"Now you are to promise me," the Marquis said, "that you will forget what I have told you, just as my servants have given me their word of honour that they will not speak of it to anybody."

He paused before he added,

"The Duchess's death will, of course, be reported in the newspapers and I will be informed by my Agent that she is dead. It is then that your brother will be able to put forward his claim and I am quite certain that there will be no difficulties about his taking his rightful place as your father's son."

"Jerry will be very – happy," Aspasia said in a low voice.

"And you? You realise you also will have a social position and a very influential one?"

There was silence and then Aspasia answered,

"I think I will be afraid of taking part in that – sort of life without Mama to guide me and – look after me.

"We will talk about it tomorrow," the Marquis suggested. "Then I will tell you what plans I am making for you."

Aspasia looked at him enquiringly and he was aware that, although she was making every effort to speak calmly and sensibly, she was still trembling and her voice when she spoke was unsteady.

He rose to his feet.

"I will take you back to your room. You will be safe now."

He thought that Aspasia would get out of bed, but instead she just stayed where she was. Then as he looked at her questioningly she said in a very small voice,

"I-I cannot – go back to that – room, you will think it very – foolish of me – but I cannot be – alone."

The Marquis did not speak and after a moment she went on,

"Perhaps I could go to – Martha – or to Uncle Theophilus?"

"I have no wish for either of them to know what has happened," the Marquis replied.

Then he smiled.

"I think, Aspasia, that the only solution is for you to stay here with me."

"Can I stay – in the same way as I – did last – night? Aspasia asked.

There was an eagerness in her voice that took away the terror that had been there before.

"It would certainly solve the problem," the Marquis said, "and I think it important that we should both have a little sleep before a new day begins."

"I will – not make you – uncomfortable?"

"I will try and bear it," the Marquis replied and she hoped that he was only teasing.

She moved as far as she could to the other side of the bed and the Marquis put a pillow in the centre of it as he had before.

He did not take off his robe, but climbed into bed on his side. As he put his head down on the pillow Aspasia stammered,

"You don't – despise me for being – such a – coward?"

"I think you have been very brave through everything that has happened," the Marquis replied. "Most women both from shock and fear would be having hysterics."

"I felt – hysterical when you were so – long in coming back." Aspasia said humbly. "I kept on imagining that Bollard might have – killed you or perhaps – you were – wounded and in pain."

Her voice told the Marquis what an agony it had been.

Then, as Aspasia recalled how the waiting had seemed like centuries and every second that ticked past had been an agony like being pierced by a dagger that grew and grew with intensity, she suddenly knew why she felt as she had.

It came to her like a revelation that was so extraordinary that she felt as if it was written on the walls in letters of fire.

It was *love* that had made her feel so agonisingly afraid, not for herself, but for the Marquis!

It was love that had made her know not only that he would save her but that, because he was the one safe bastion in her little world, she could not lose him. When he had left the room her fear was a thousand times more intense and more terrifying because she had been thinking not of herself but of him.

Of course it was love, but she had not realised it, that made her know that if he was killed there would be a despairing sense of loss which she knew her mother must have felt when the Duke had been drowned.

'I love him in the – same way,' Aspasia told herself.

She lay staring into the darkness, pulsatingly aware that the Marquis was not dead but beside her.

*

Aspasia awoke and for a moment could not think what had happened.

Then she saw the sunshine streaming through the curtains and was aware that she was not beside the Marquis in his bed as she expected but in her own bedroom.

She knew that he must have carried her back, perhaps when dawn broke, and she realised that he had been safe-guarding her against anybody knowing where she had spent the night.

She found it hard to believe that he had carried her without her waking, but she supposed that she had slept the deep sleep of exhaustion. It had inevitably followed the dramatic events of yesterday, while she had gone to bed very late the night before as well.

'How could so much have happened in so short a time?' Aspasia asked herself. "But the Marquis has saved us – saved us – all!"

To think of him was to feel as if she saw him in front of her eyes enveloped in rays of light.

Then a thought came to her that made her sit up apprehensively as if she wanted to go to him and ask him to reassure her.

Now that she and Jerry were no longer menaced by the Duchess, the Marquis would feel that he was free of their problems and perhaps she would not see him anymore.

He would, of course, take an interest in Jerry's claim to the Dukedom, but that would be put forward quite easily by a Solicitor, Aspasia thought, now that they could afford one.

Anyway it was a legal matter that she would play no part in

'He will leave me and I shall never see him again,' Aspasia told herself gloomily.

She climbed out of bed because she could not bear to waste a moment away from the Marquis when she might be with him.

'I must remember everything he says and try to persuade him to help me as long as possible before he finds me – nothing but a – bore.'

It was agony to think of his disappearing out of her life and yet she knew that it was inevitable.

When she and Jerry had watched the Marquis's horses win, she had learnt not only that he was a great sportsman but that he was constantly with the Prince Regent, a member of the Jockey Club, and obviously a very consequential figure in Society.

Her mother, when speaking of the Duke, had explained to her the life that was led by a Nobleman and there had been people in Little Medlock who had described the entertainment that had taken place at Grimstone before the old Duchess had been taken ill.

When she saw the house, it had been easy for Aspasia to understand how glamorous and impressive such parties had been.

Jerry would be able to entertain in the same way, but Aspasia thought that he would be more interested in the horses he could possess and perhaps in owning a yacht like the one the Marquis boasted.

'But what will become of me?' she wondered.

She would be lost and lonely, and perhaps it would be best for her to live at the Vicarage with Uncle Theophilus who, now the Duchess was dead, would not lose the Parish he loved so much.

Martha came to help her dress and Aspasia thought despairingly that she had only the same riding habit to wear and the Marquis would hardly be likely to admire her when she looked dowdy and unlike the beautiful women who must be his companions in London.

She had slept so late that she had breakfast in her bedroom and when she was dressed she went downstairs having learned from Martha that the Marquis intended them to leave soon after eleven o'clock.

Martha did not know where they were going, and Aspasia was suddenly afraid that he was sending her and Uncle Theophilus back to the Vicarage.

There was no reason for him to take care of them any longer and Aspasia was sure that now there was no longer any danger he would merely find her an encumbrance.

Nevertheless, when she entered the Marquis's study where the butler had told her he was waiting, she felt when she saw him it was as if the room was suddenly enveloped with a celestial light.

When she smiled at her, she felt as if it was so dazzling that she was blinded by it.

"Good morning, Aspasia."

"I-I am afraid I slept very – late."

"You were naturally very tired."

"I did not wake when you – carried me – back to my – room."

"I made every effort to make sure that you did not do so," the Marquis smiled. "But now I hope you are ready to leave. We have a long distance to go."

Aspasia looked at him enquiringly and afraid to ask for an explanation.

"I am taking you to Thame," the Marquis said, "for reasons I will explain later. But in case you are worried, let me tell you that the precious box belonging to your mother has already left for London."

Aspasia made an exclamation of delight and he went on,

"I have given my Agent instructions for it to be deposited with my family Solicitors, who will deal most adequately with all the legal aspects of your brother's case."

"Oh, thank you," Aspasia answered. "You are so kind – and I knew that you would know exactly what to do."

"I am glad that you and Jerry should trust me," the Marquis said.

"Of course we do," Aspasia replied.

She wondered what he would say if she added that she loved him, that even to look at him was making her heart beat in a very strange manner and it was hard to speak as well.

Then she told herself that she had to face the fact that she would merely embarrass the Marquis if he had the slightest idea that her feelings were in any way intimate.

She was certain that he looked upon her as a rather tiresome child whom he had helped and saved because it was his duty as a gentleman to do so.

"Why are we going to – Thame?" she asked.

"That is something I was going to explain to you," the Marquis said, "and I hope it will meet with your approval."

"Everything will meet with my approval as long – as I can go with you."

There was such a lilt in her voice and a light in her eyes that the Marquis for the moment seemed surprised.

"What I am going to suggest," he said, "is that you and I ride across country, which is much the quickest way, while your uncle, your maid and your luggage go by road, which will take well over an hour longer."

"My – luggage?" Aspasia questioned.

"I sent to the Vicarage for it earlier this morning, before you were awake," the Marquis said. "Your clothes, your uncle's and your maid's arrived here about fifteen minutes ago."

Aspasia clasped her hands together.

"How can you be so – fantastic?" she asked. "How can you think of – everything?"

"I try to," the Marquis replied, "and if Charlie was here he would tell you that organisation is something that I have always found interesting. So I hope that you will think that Thame, if nothing else, is well organised."

Before she reached Thame, Aspasia found that the Marquis's organising ability extended to providing them with an excellent luncheon at a small wayside inn.

They had ridden for about an hour and a half before they reached it, where the landlord, a large jovial man, welcomed them effusively and took them into a small garden at the side of the inn where a table had been laid under a weeping willow tree.

The garden was unkempt, but it was filled with the simple flowers that reminded Aspasia of the cottages in Little Medlock.

There were marigolds and pansies, roses and forget-me-nots and she thought to herself that because she was alone with the Marquis it was like being in a small Garden of Eden in which nobody else could encroach.

It was a simple luncheon augmented with dishes supplied by the Marquis's chef in Newmarket, but served by a buxom young woman in a mob cap instead of one of the Marquis's liveried staff.

"You remembered my lemonade!" Aspasia exclaimed.

"Of course," the Marquis replied. "I try to remember everything you like and dislike."

"I like being here," Aspasia smiled. "It is so pretty and so simple, and not – frightening."

The Marquis was about to say something about her being frightened. Then he changed his mind and soon they were riding on over fields and through woods.

To Aspasia it was not only a wonderful experience to be with the Marquis but also to ride a horse which was finer than anything she had ever had the chance of riding before and was trained to respond to her every touch.

"I have wanted to see you on a horse," the Marquis said unexpectedly. "I had a feeling that you would be a very good rider."

"I have only ridden horses in the past that Jerry and I bought at the Horse Fairs or from farmers and broke in ourselves."

"That is something you will never have to do again."

The Marquis had intended that his remark should give her pleasure, but Aspasia thought he meant that she would be living at Grimstone with Jerry and would be able to ride the horses in his stable.

But she knew that the finest horses in the world would not compensate for not being with the Marquis and not being able to ride beside him as she was doing now.

She looked at him from under her eyelashes, thinking that it would be impossible for any man to look more handsome or to ride better.

She had always thought that Jerry was a good rider, but the Marquis seemed part of his horse and he rode with an expertise that Aspasia could see was exceptional.

They did not talk much after luncheon, but rode for another hour and a half until the Marquis pointed with his whip and said,

"There is Thame!"

Standing on a rising piece of ground with woods behind it and a large lake in front it looked to Aspasia like a Fairy Palace.

If Grimstone had been impressive, Thame was serenely beautiful, and its turrets and towers silhouetted against the sky made her feel that it was not real but part of a dream.

As they rode down the drive, she felt a pang of despair because in a few minutes she would no longer be alone with the Marquis. There would be his servants and within the hour Uncle Theophilus would arrive.

Impulsively she said,

"Thank you for letting me ride here with – you. It was something I shall always remember."

"You speak as if it will not happen again," the Marquis observed.

"I hope it – will," Aspasia said in a low voice, "but I realise that you are a very busy person – and I have no wish to be a – nuisance."

"You have not been that since I first met you," the Marquis said. "A surprise, a problem, a deep anxiety, but never a nuisance or a bore, Aspasia!"

She felt that he must have been reading her thoughts.

"That is what I – wanted you to say, for it is – something I am – very afraid of."

They were drawing nearer to the front of the house and she added,

"Please – you must tell me when you – wish me to go – away. I would not want to outstay my – welcome like some guests who – never know when to leave."

The Marquis laughed.

"Who told you that?"

"It is what I have often thought when people call to see Uncle Theophilus," Aspasia replied. "They stay and stay! There seems to be no polite way of getting rid of them."

She smiled.

"I am sure you would be able to turn them out without their even being aware that you wanted them to go!"

"I promise I will let you know if you are unwelcome."

"Thank – you," Aspasia replied and hoped in her heart that it would be a long, long time before it happened.

They went into the house, which she felt had a different atmosphere from any house that she had been in before.

She could not explain it to herself, but it was as if she felt vibrations of happiness coming towards her and there was too a feeling of security as if the walls were like arms enfolding her and holding her close.

She had wanted to see the Marquis's pictures and now they were there, magnificent and entrancing.

Almost before she was inside a room she found herself giving exclamations of delight at what she saw hanging on the walls.

The Marquis looked at her with a smile before he said,

"I want to talk to you, Aspasia, before your uncle arrives."

She looked at him apprehensively.

It had been hot while they were riding and now she had pulled off her riding hat and put it down on a chair.

Then after a moment's hesitation she took off her riding jacket.

Martha had washed and pressed her white blouse last night, but Aspasia thought that it must look very dull and dowdy compared to everything in the Marquis's magnificent house.

Then she forgot it as she walked towards him and saw that he was watching her.

She reached his side and looked up at him enquiringly guessing that he had something important to say, but immediately feeling apprehensive in case it was something she did not wish to hear.

She sensed that the Marquis was feeling for words.

Then he said,

"Last night before you came to my room I had been considering your future."

Aspasia stiffened.

She was quite certain that this was going to be something that would make her unhappy.

"There is – no reason why you should – trouble about me – now."

"You have plans of your own?" the Marquis enquired.

"I was thinking when we were riding here," Aspasia said in a small voice, "that it would be – best for me to go back to the – Vicarage and look after Uncle Theophilus – as I have done ever since – Mama died."

The Marquis looked at her as if to reassure himself that she was speaking sincerely and then he said,

"I think that, if nothing else, would be a waste of your looks."

"M-my – looks?" Aspasia asked in astonishment.

"You must be aware that you are very beautiful."

The Marquis spoke in his usual, quiet dry voice and went on,

"When I first saw you, I thought that in London, even amongst the great beauties to be found there, you would cause a sensation."

"You – thought that when you – saw me at – Grimstone House?"

The Marquis's eyes twinkled.

"I was not exactly visualising you at Carlton House or Buckingham Palace," he said, "but I know now that wherever you were you would be acclaimed and complimented."

"Thank – you," Aspasia answered, "but as you are well aware – it would only – frighten me and I don't want to – receive compliments from – "

She could not find the right word, but the Marquis knew as he watched her that she was thinking of the men who had been at the dinner party given by the Duchess.

She had been astonished and disgusted by their behaviour, yet she was aware that they were aristocrats who bore distinguished titles.

"The men you saw the other night," he said, "are not, thank God, representative of the majority of those who are born gentlemen."

He spoke sharply and Aspasia replied,

"Please – I do *not* – wish to enter – Society. Jerry will be happy because he will be among the friends he met at Oxford – but I shall know – nobody."

"Except me!"

Aspasia looked up at the Marquis and found it hard to look away.

His eyes seemed to hold hers captive and there was a silence while they just gazed at each other before he said,

"You would not be afraid with me?"

"No – of course not! I am never – afraid with you. Actually it is only when I am with – you that I feel – safe."

"In which case I feel that you will find it easy to accept my plan for your future."

"What – is it?" Aspasia asked in a whisper.

"That you should marry me!"

For a moment she felt that she could not have heard him aright.

Then, as she stared at him, her eyes seeming to fill her whole face, he put his arms around her and drew her close against him.

"I will protect you and you will never be afraid again," he said very quietly.

Then his lips were on hers.

CHAPTER SEVEN

For a moment Aspasia was too astonished to feel anything but surprise.

Then the strength of the Marquis's arms around her and the insistence of his lips on hers made her feel a strange, wild inexplicable sensation that she had never known before.

It seemed to rise from her breasts into her throat and from her throat into her lips so that as the Marquis's kiss grew more insistent she felt as if she became a part of him.

It swept away her fears and everything else but an ecstatic rapture.

He drew her closer still and, as his lips became more demanding and more possessive, Aspasia knew that this was what, without being aware of it, she had always longed for and dreamed about.

This was love, the love she had discovered last night, but more perfect, more marvellous and more Divine.

After what might have been a few minutes or a century of time, the Marquis raised his head to look down at her.

He thought that, with her eyes wide and shining, her lips warm and rosy from his kisses and her hair flaming like fire against his arm, she was more beautiful than any woman he had ever seen in his whole life.

"I love – you!" Aspasia whispered.

"Are you sure of that?"

"Very – very sure," she replied. "But it was only last – night that I – realised what I – felt for you was – *love*."

"And now what do you feel for me?" he asked her.

"That you are – magnificent – so magnificent that I could not think of you as – somebody I could – love."

"But you do love me?"

"I did not – know that I could – feel like – this and that it was love."

The Marquis kissed her again.

Then, as he felt her quivering against him, but not with fear, he knew that the sensations she aroused in him were different from anything he had ever felt before.

When she could finally speak, Aspasia said,

"Do you – really mean – that I can – marry you?"

"I have every intention of making you my wife."

"But – how – how can you – marry me when there are so many other – women that you could ask?"

"I have never asked any other woman to marry me," the Marquis replied. "And this is the truth, Aspasia, I never wished to be married until now."

"How can you – want me?"

The Marquis thought that there were a hundred answers he could give her, but instead with a faint smile he said,

"One good reason is because I cannot go on having sleepless nights with a pillow keeping us apart."

"I kept you – awake?" Aspasia asked with a note of concern in her voice. "I hoped I was – very quiet."

"You were but I found it impossible to sleep when you were so near to me."

He saw in her innocence that she did not understand and added,

"I will explain why later on tonight."

"Tonight?" Aspasia questioned.

"After we are married."

Her eyes widened and he saw sheer astonishment in them.

"I have already arranged it with your uncle," he said, "and when he arrives he will marry us in my private Chapel. Early this morning I sent to London for a Special Licence and I expect it will be here by now."

"Tonight?" Aspasia whispered.

"There are many reasons for that too," the Marquis said, "besides the pillow between us."

"What are – they?"

"First because I want you to belong to me and I want to make sure that I can protect you from your own fears," the Marquis answered. "Secondly because although your uncle could be here to chaperone you, I think it important that he should return to Little Medlock to look after Jerry's interests."

He knew by the expression on Aspasia's face that she understood that once it was known that the Duchess was dead, Mrs. Fielding and the other disreputable servants she had employed might steal or damage the treasures in the house that now belonged to Jerry.

"Everything is arranged," the Marquis went on. "As soon as news of the Duchess's death reaches Newmarket, my Agent has my instructions to proceed immediately to Grimstone House with the local Solicitors."

Aspasia made a little murmur of gratitude.

"They will take charge of everything," he continued, "and will make an inventory of the house's contents. I know that your uncle when he arrives, because he is so respected in the neighbourhood, will see that those who are no longer wanted on the estate will leave immediately."

"You have thought of – everything!" Aspasia exclaimed as she had done before.

"I try to, but at the moment I am finding it difficult to think of anything but you."

"It is hard to – believe that – you really – love me."

"I will make you believe it."

"I think – I really am – dreaming," Aspasia said. "Dreaming of my love for you and that – you love me and dreaming that I need no – longer be – afraid."

She gave a little shiver as she added,

"I think I have been – afraid all my life – but especially so since I – went to – Grimstone House."

"When you go there again, it will be a very different place."

"You will – come with – me?"

"Not only to Grimstone House," the Marquis answered, "but everywhere else. I know, my darling, that you need me just as I need you."

"I do need you. I need you – desperately!" Aspasia cried. "Now you are holding me in your arms I am not afraid, but, although you will think it very – foolish, I will be – afraid, terribly – afraid if ever – I am alone."

"That is what I am here to prevent," the Marquis said as he kissed her again..

He thought as he did so that few women would be so courageous and so sensible after all she had been through.

At the same time he was perceptive enough to know that the horrors of the last few days would take a long time to erase from Aspasia's mind.

The only way that could be done completely was to give her something else to think about and what could be more effective than love?

Actually he found it very hard to believe that he should have fallen in love so completely and so overwhelmingly when he had so confidently believed that it was something that would never happen to him.

He had known that first night at Grimstone House that Aspasia was different from anybody he had met before.

When he had finally realised how pure and innocent she was, he had thought that she was unique not only for her beauty but for her character and personality.

Yet some hard cynical part of his brain told him that a young girl who lived in a Vicarage and knew nothing of the world he moved in could mean nothing in his busy well-organised life.

He was so confident that he was complete in himself.

Yet when he had ridden away from the Vicarage having left Aspasia there, he had the uncontrollable feeling that he was losing something precious and something sublime that he might never find again.

It was his brain that had laughed at him for being foolish, his brain which made him return to Newmarket after he had seen the Duchess

But a very different part of him was urging him to see Aspasia once more to make sure that she was as different from all the other women he had ever known as he had found her to be.

He had thought about her all the time he was riding back to where Charlie was waiting for him.

He kept telling himself that what had happened was just one episode in his life that he would doubtless remember with amusement and that the Duchess's outrageous behaviour was something that really was not his concern.

But all the time he was telling Charlie what had happened at Grimstone House he could see Aspasia's frightened blue eyes and feel her trembling as she had when he put his arm around her to take her from the dining room.

When she had arrived unexpectedly and walked into the study, he felt first an irrepressible joy and then a very different feeling which, he admitted later, was jealousy because she was accompanied by a man.

After Aspasia asked for his help and he saw how terrified she was of what was happening at the Vicarage, he had known that there was no escape for him nor did he wish for one for his life was now indivisibly woven with hers forever.

With his usual acute perception, however, the Marquis was well aware that he must not frighten her more than she was frightened already.

He was also still listening to some extent to the warnings of his brain that told him that it would be a great mistake to act precipitately and that whatever he might feel about Aspasia he was too old and far too sophisticated to be the husband of a young girl.

Then last night when Aspasia had rushed into his bedroom to fling herself against him and later when he returned to find her almost frantic with fear that he had been killed or wounded he admitted that he was deeply wildly and irrevocably in love.

Because the Marquis had great self-discipline and because he had known that her experiences had been traumatic in a manner that would make it difficult for her to think clearly, he had behaved, as he told himself faintly mockingly, 'like a perfect gentleman'.

Yet it had been an agony not to kiss Aspasia and, when she asked if she could stay with him, not to hold her in his arms all night.

For the first time in his life the Marquis was thinking of a woman rather than of himself and he had lain awake making plans that he believed would make Aspasia happy.

Now he knew by the radiance in her face that he had taken the right decision and that his instinct had not failed him.

Aspasia looked into his eyes for one moment and then she gave a little murmur of contentment and put her head against his shoulder.

The Marquis sensed that she had no wish to leave the shelter of his arms and he kissed her hair before he said,

"You are not to worry, my darling, Just leave everything to me. I promise you that now everything will be all right."

"Are you – bringing Jerry – home?"

"Seeing how excited he was at the thought of a sea voyage and knowing it is what Charlie enjoys too, I thought it might be a good idea for the yacht to reach Plymouth before I tell them to return."

He was aware that Aspasia was wondering if there was another reason for this and he added,

"I also felt that you would have no wish for Jerry to be involved in any way with the women or the servants we saw at Grimstone House."

"No – of course not!" Aspasia cried.

"They will be turned out and because it will be his home I want him to see it as it must have been in your father's time, a house of happiness that decent people will be eager to be invited to visit."

"You are so clever to think like – that," Aspasia said. "It is just what Mama would – want."

"When we come back from our honeymoon," the Marquis went on, "we will both help Jerry to put things straight and we will also together ensure that he meets the best of London Society and not the members of it who would be a bad influence on him."

"That is what Mama would have wanted too! Oh, how can I have been so lucky to have found you?"

"I think you were the one responsible for that," the Marquis smiled.

"I was so – frightened," Aspasia answered, "terrified of what you might be – like, but now I know that it was God or – Mama who sent me to – Grimstone House. Otherwise we would – never have – met."

"God certainly moves in mysterious ways," the Marquis commented a little dryly, "but I agree, my precious one, that Fate has been very kind to us. And now that I have found you I will never let you go and that is why I intend to marry you, Aspasia."

"You are quite – quite certain it is – what you – should do?" she asked. "Suppose you regret having married me and find me too – stupid and – ignorant to keep you – interested?"

"You already know some of the things that I find interesting," the Marquis replied. "For instance you know a great deal about my horses, my pictures and I am looking forward more than I can tell you to showing you my other possessions."

"I shall – love that."

"I will teach you about the other things that interest me," the Marquis continued, "which at the moment is only *you*."

He pulled her against him and kissed her until Aspasia felt that her feet were no longer on the ground and the Marquis was carrying her high into the sky, where his lips had the fire of the sun in them.

It was so perfect and so wonderful that it flashed through her mind that if she should die now she would have had everything in life that mattered and there was nothing that could be more perfect or more wonderful than love.

Then she knew that she wanted to live and to tell the Marquis how much she loved him over and over again.

She was trying in vain to find words to express the glory and the wonder that was within her when she heard the door of the study open and saw that her uncle had arrived.

*

Later the Marquis took Aspasia upstairs to her room.

She wanted to look round her because there were so many things that she wanted to see. At the same time, because he was beside her, it was impossible to think of anything but him.

He took her by the hand and led her up the stairs and she knew that the touch of his fingers thrilled her and she could only look at him thinking that no man could be more handsome, more distinguished and more wonderful.

'I love you! *I love you!*' she wanted to say and keep on saying it, but she thought shyly that he might think that she was being too effusive.

They walked along a broad corridor and, when the Marquis opened a door, Aspasia was aware that they were in a room that was part of the Master suite.

"All the Marchionesses of Thame have slept here," the Marquis told her.

After Aspasia had expressed her delight that Martha was there waiting for her, she was able to look around.

The room was beautiful, the walls decorated in white, picked out in gold with panels of blue brocade that were the colour of her eyes.

As she thought of it, she saw that the Marquis was smiling and knew that he was aware of what she was thinking.

"The room might have been decorated for you," he said, "but actually it was designed nearly a hundred years ago."

"It is very beautiful," Aspasia sighed, looking up at the ceiling painted with cupids and Goddesses whose colours echoed those of the Aubusson carpet on the floor.

But what made the colour flood into her cheeks was the bed with its gold corolla from which hung curtains of exquisite lace over blue silk that matched the panels on the wall.

The Marquis watched her eyes, but he said nothing until he raised her hand to his lips.

"Your uncle will be ready to marry us in an hour's time," he said quietly and went from the room.

Aspasia turned to Martha to see that she was crying.

"I've never been so happy in all me life, Miss Aspasia!" she sobbed. It's what your dear mother would have wanted for you, but I never thought it'd ever happen livin' as we were at Little Medlock with nothin' but the cabbages to talk to!"

Aspasia laughed.

"Oh, Martha, how funny you are. But I too think Mama would have been happy that I should marry such a wonderful man."

"I can hardly believe it's true," Martha said, "and what'll Master Jerry have to say when he hears of it? It'll upset him not to be at your Wedding."

With difficulty Aspasia realised that she must not let Martha know yet that Jerry would have a great many other things to think about besides herself.

Instead she said,

"I want to be married, Martha. At the same time I wish I had a beautiful Wedding gown."

She thought as she spoke of the white snowdrop gown she had worn at Grimstone House, but she knew that attractive though it was, it was symbolic of all that was evil and bad.

She could not contemplate for a moment wearing it at a Ceremony that was sacred.

Martha blew her nose and put away her handkerchief.

"Didn't his Lordship tell you that you've a Wedding gown waitin' for you, Miss Aspasia?"

Aspasia looked at her questioningly and Martha crossed the room to open the door of a beautiful inlaid and gilt-ornamented cupboard.

Inside, hanging beside some of her simple dresses that Martha had made, was a white gown that was both fashionable and beautiful.

Martha took it out of the cupboard and held it up for her to see and Aspasia gave a gasp of surprise. Trimmed with fine lace over pure white silk it seemed as if, like the house itself, it had stepped straight from a Fairytale.

"Oh – Martha – !" Aspasia exclaimed.

"I didn't know when his Lordship asks me last night for your measurements," Martha said, "that he were thinkin' of anythin' like this!"

"It is p-part of his – b-brilliant organisation," Aspasia stammered.

She told herself that he was not only the most efficient man in the world but also the kindest and the most thoughtful.

'How could he have guessed,' she asked, 'that much as I love him, my Wedding would not have been perfect if I felt that I was not elegant and smart enough for him?'

When she had had a bath, Martha dressed her in the lace gown and she found that there was a family veil to wear over her head and a diamond tiara which made her gasp when she opened the box that it was displayed in.

Perhaps this more than anything else made Aspasia realise that when she was married to the Marquis she would be a Marchioness and socially elevated.

Things would be expected of her that she was afraid she might not be capable of doing.

When she was ready, she went downstairs to where she knew that the Marquis was waiting for her and Martha said as if she knew what she was feeling,

"Your mother, God bless her, will be in the Chapel today, lovin' you and she's always there should you need her."

Her words dispersed a little shadow that for the moment dimmed Aspasia's happiness.

"Thank you, Martha," she said, "and thank you for looking after Jerry and me all these years when things have been so difficult."

She saw the tears come into the old maid's eyes.

Martha quickly bustled away so that she could be in the Chapel before the bride and bridegroom reached it.

As Aspasia walked down the staircase, she saw the Marquis waiting for her.

He watched her descending slowly step by step, very conscious of the veil enveloping her and the tiara shining on her red-gold hair.

When she reached him, she thought that there was an expression in his eyes that she had not seen before.

He did not speak, he only gave her his arm and drew her down a long corridor to where at the end of it there was the Private Chapel.

Because her arm was through his and because he put his hand over hers, Aspasia was vibrating to him as if to beautiful music.

Her heart was beating frantically because he was so close to her and because the wonder of knowing that she was to be his wife made her feel as if the gates of Heaven were opening.

As they knelt side by side in the Chapel and her uncle blessed them, Aspasia knew that not only was her mother beside her, but that a celestial light enveloped them that came from God.

Martha looked around the bedroom to see that everything was tidy and then she blew out the candles on the dressing table and walked towards the door.

"Goodnight and God bless you," she said as she had said every night since Aspasia was a child.

"Goodnight – Martha."

It was hard to say the words or to realise that she was not in her little bed in the Vicarage where she had slept all her life.

Instead she was in the most beautiful room that she had ever seen in a bed that could only have belonged to a Princess in a Fairytale.

And she was waiting for the Marquis.

He came in through the communicating door, which, she had learned, led into his bedroom and she thought that it was impossible for any man to look happier.

He came quietly across the carpet and stood for a moment looking down at her before he sat on the side of the bed.

"This is what I have been waiting for all day, my darling," he began, "and I feel as if I have in fact waited an Eternity."

"We are – married. We are really – married!" Aspasia said as if she would convince herself.

"We are married," the Marquis repeated in a deep voice, "and tonight, my beloved, there will be no pillow between us."

Aspasia gave him a shy little smile.

Then she said,

"There is – something I want to – say to – you."

"You are not worried about anything?" he asked quickly.

"Only – about what I have to – say."

"What is it?"

The Marquis looked down at her fingers and saw that she was twisting them together as if she was nervous.

"My darling," he said quickly, "I will not frighten you."

"I-I am not frightened of you," Aspasia replied. "It is just that – I am afraid – because I am so – ignorant."

She did not wait for the Marquis to speak, but went on quickly,

"S-supposing that I do – something that is – wrong and then you don't – love me any m-more?"

The Marquis reached out and put his hand over hers.

He felt her fingers tremble as if he held a small bird in his grasp.

"My precious little wife," he sighed. "There is nothing you could do that would be wrong unless you no longer loved me."

"I love you! *I love you!*" Aspasia answered. "I love you so – much that you fill the – whole world and the sky – there is nothing – else but – *you*."

The Marquis's fingers tightened on hers, but otherwise he did not move.

"But still you are afraid."

"Only that I shall – fail you in some way – supposing you are – disappointed that you have m-married me?"

"I am quite certain I shall not be that," he said, but Aspasia was following the train of her thoughts.

"You said – I know about your interests – but I know – nothing about – love or what a man – wants from a – woman."

The Marquis thought that she was thinking of the behaviour of the men and women at Grimstone House and the naked actors and actresses on the stage.

He drew in his breath thinking that in all his numerous affairs he had never had to explain love or teach it.

But because Aspasia was so different and because he knew that her shyness came from a purity that he had never found before, he felt that his love almost overwhelmed him in its intensity.

He knew now that what he felt for her was not just the desire of a man for an attractive woman but something so spiritual and so essentially good that it was impossible for him to express it.

He only knew that he wanted to look after her, to protect her and love her so that never again would he see an expression either of fear or disgust in her eyes.

Now he said very quietly,

"This evening when we were married, my darling, I vowed that I will love adore and worship you all our lives and will continue to do so in the life to come."

The Marquis was astonished at his own words, and yet they came from his heart.

Then he saw a light come into Aspasia's eyes and her fingers no longer trembled on his.

"You are so – wonderful!" she exclaimed. "How could I do – anything but – worship you?"

"I think, my precious one," the Marquis said, "that all we have to do is listen to our hearts and love will show us the way."

As he spoke, he put his arms around Aspasia and his lips found hers.

He kissed her very gently until he felt her respond and then, as he went on kissing her, he knew that he was igniting a little flame within her.

Then Aspasia said with a note of passion in her voice that he had never heard before,

"I love – you and I – want to be – closer and closer – to you so that I can – can tell you how much I – love you and I am – no longer afraid – because I am in your arms."

The Marquis took off his robe and climbed into the bed and, as Aspasia moved closer to him and he felt her body warm against his, he thought that he did not know such happiness existed.

Looking up at him in the dim light of the candles shining through the lace curtains, she said,

"This is – how I wanted – us to be last night – but I – thought you would be very – shocked if I moved – next to you."

"If you only knew how much I wanted it too," the Marquis replied, "but now, my precious darling, we are married and I can hold you close and even closer."

"I want to be – very – very close," Aspasia whispered, "but when you kiss me – it is so exciting that – it is difficult – to breathe."

She gave a little sigh.

"It is – impossible to explain – but please – teach me about love – and make me love you as you – want to be loved."

"That is what I intend to do," the Marquis said and his voice was very deep and a little unsteady. "And this, my adorable one, is your first lesson."

Then he was kissing her again, kissing her lips, until his mouth moved to the softness of her neck.

Aspasia felt a sensation like a shaft of lightning streak through her and her breath came in little gasps.

"I – love you – *Oh – I love – you*!"

The Marquis pulled aside her nightgown and kissed her breasts and then again her lips until she put up her hands in protest.

"I am not frightening you, my precious?" he asked hoarsely.

"No – but you – make me feel – so – strange."

"In what way?"

"As – if – there is a fire burning – inside me but I also – want you to kiss me – and go on – kissing me more and more – but still it – is not enough."

"My sweet perfect little wife."

The Marquis held her mouth captive, his hand was touching her and the flames in Aspasia leapt higher and higher.

It was no longer possible to think or to be afraid.

All she knew was that the Marquis was lifting her into the sky, the gates of Heaven were open and, as they entered them together, they were one for all Eternity.

OTHER BOOKS IN THIS SERIES

The Barbara Cartland Eternal Collection is the unique opportunity to collect all five hundred of the timeless beautiful romantic novels written by the world's most celebrated and enduring romantic author.

Named the Eternal Collection because Barbara's inspiring stories of pure love, just the same as love itself, the books will be published on the internet at the rate of four titles per month until all five hundred are available.

The Eternal Collection, classic pure romance available worldwide for all time.